# LETHAL TRAIL

## NO BODY IS SAFE

A SAM TRAVIS ADVENTURE

# GK JURRENS

# LT. TOM KASPRZAK (RETIRED)

UpLife
Press

*Please note the list of major characters
in the appendix*

**Subscribe at GKJurrens.com**, *and don't forget to leave a brief review
on Amazon. Or email gjurrens@yahoo.com with your comments. We'd
love to hear from you. Thanks!*

*- GK & TK*

# INTRODUCTION

LETHAL TRAIL is based on actual cases from the annals of Massachusetts Law Enforcement. We have attempted to be true to the spirit of these cases, to officers of the law who investigated and prosecuted them, and especially to their victims.

This is fiction, but has not been watered down. So, we depict a handful of scenes that contain graphic violence in an effort not only to deliver an entertaining tale of crime and justice, but to convey what real victims of real crimes experience—physically and emotionally.

We do not apologize for this true-to-life portrayal of the darker side of humanity, but we ask you to revel in the uplifting courage and perseverance of victims, citizens who help victims, and officers of the law who not only seek justice, but deliver hope for a better future according to the rule of law.

# 1

Triple-digit heat and absurd humidity stifled life the summer of 1972. Grit filled the air. Every breath came hard. Not a single leaf wavered on any tree. The entire valley, including the industrial city of Karamusell, Pennsylvania, cooked on a slow boil. While moisture clung to every clammy surface, rain refused to fall. But that wasn't the worst of it.

Unlike the much larger Bethlehem, one large mill in the small steel-producing community provided a livelihood for forty-thousand souls of its seventy-thousand population. The work was dirty and unmerciful, even in the winter. The mill's furnaces ran at four-thousand-five hundred degrees. Roads shimmered like mirages in the desert and heaved humps in the hottest spots. Most men here spent their entire adult lives in this hell on earth. The pay was okay at *American Steel*, but many exchanged it for their health.

Tract homes sprouted everywhere—carbon copies. These ugly little thousand-square-foot coffins for the barely living comprised three small bedrooms, one full bath, a small living room, and an even smaller eat-in kitchen. They all squatted on a one-hundred-by-one-hundred-foot postage stamp lot. Only a few featured a tree or a couple of small bushes. No garages, no driveways, no curbs, no gutters.

In the early days, the working conditions at *American Steel* fell nothing short of slave labor. Men toiled in Hell twelve hours a day, seven days a week, with the Fourth of July as their only holiday. Union strikes, political pressure and some weak legislation helped to improve conditions, but not much.

Liam's dear old dad, Michael Sullivan, worked at *American*. Fifteen years earlier, he had married Elsa Lannigan, also a second-generation immigrant.

That was before the Irish. Their two sons—Liam, twelve and Mac, eight—attended the same school. Of almost six-hundred students, ninety percent were sons and daughters of *American Steel* workers. Liam and Mac were good kids. When they got in trouble, Michael administered ten healthy whacks on a bare butt with the thick black strap that hung over the water heater in the kitchen.

Michael had always been a powerful man, like most steel workers. The boys feared him, and Ma just stayed out of his way. He customarily grew sullen and unapproachable once home from the mill. Just wanted to eat, park his ass in his favorite recliner, and drink his Irish whiskey until he blacked out in front of the TV. The boys also knew to steer clear of the old man after his fourth stiff belt. So did Ma. Even though he didn't beat her, he broke her down.

The heat would relent soon, with a cold front sweeping down from the northwest. That would bring strong thunderstorms and cooler weather. At least that was the prediction, that they'd sleep better. Even with every window open, the house was a sauna. The old man roared that he hated the stink of the mill that clung to him day and night. Said as much. Every night. Not even a cool bath could rid him of that awful stench of melting steel. The whole family knew the Irish helped.

Then, Liam's hormones kicked in—a confusing time. Younger brother Mac was still a little boy. They got along because they had to. There'd be hell to pay if Ma ratted them out to their dad for some misadventure. Liam was not an athlete, but he possessed the genetic predisposition of his father's physicality, who was five-foot-ten and two-hundred pounds. Big and tough as a bull. Mean, too, after a few belts of the Irish.

Liam—ever bashful—became aware of girls, but remained reluctant to engage with them. At almost thirteen, he grew like a weed, and challenged the family's already strained food budget. The school gym at St. Stevens, a combined middle and high school, sported an indoor basketball court. Thanks to grants from *American* over the years, the school also featured a small baseball field, a football practice field, student showers, and most important to Liam, a decent weight room.

Later, in high school, Liam was no athlete and didn't want to be, but he was drawn to that weight room. He lifted weights to attract girls. He knew most girls liked muscular boys. Neither ugly nor handsome, he possessed a strong brow, but a weak chin. He figured a good build might get the girls to take a second look in his direction, even if he didn't know how to talk to them. But then, everything changed.

# 2

So it had begun. By 1977, Liam was spending every moment possible on the machines and free weights in the gym at St. Stevens. His grades suffered, and he heard about it from Ma. His dad didn't give a shit. After several months he began to bulk out. In his junior year of high school he met another boy—Conor. No last name—a runt from Coal Town. He too, was a bit scrawny and not handsome, but possessed the same goals as Liam. They were the same age but in different classes. Liam remembered how they had met.

Once while bench pressing a hundred-fifty pounds, Liam saw Conor turning blue from a barbell across his wind pipe. Liam rushed to his aid and lifted the bar off Conor's throat. "Guess you need a spotter with that kind of weight."

Conor responded after a few labored breaths. "Thanks. I thought I could get in one more rep. Hey, how 'bout I spot for you? We could workout together?" Liam was reticent at first, but needed and wanted a friend, someone with whom to talk about these crazy feelings in his loins that felt like ignited napalm on his balls.

They became friends. By their senior year, neither one had yet dated. Both remained bashful and unsure of themselves. Both only speculated how to go about getting a girl. Hanging with the varsity boys in the weight room, they overheard stories of banging cheerleaders. That made Liam jealous and angry. "I'm gonna ask Ginny." She was a cheerleader, and his favorite.

"Ask her what?"

"Seriously, Conor?" Ginny was pretty, outgoing and popular—green eyes, blond hair and a babe's figure. When he thought of getting naked with her —instant erection.

He rehearsed his lines. After school, Liam caught up with Ginny Swanson as she walked home. "Hi, I'm Liam. We're in the same history class."

Ginny looked at him and smiled. "Hey, Liam."

Encouraged, he pressed on. He had little money, but had saved up enough for two ice cream sodas by picking up and redeeming nickel Coke bottles along the road home. "Would you like to come with me over to Vernon Street Drugstore for an ice cream soda?"

"No thanks. I've got to babysit and I already have a boyfriend. And honestly, I don't think you're my type."

Deflated, he struggled with what to say next. After another dozen steps, "Well, I don't know what type you're looking for, but whatever it is, I can be that for you."

"Liam, you seem nice. But I hate Karamusell and want out of this shit-hole of a town. I need to be with someone who will get me away from this place. And I want a nice house, with a garden, and a man who can make enough money to support me. I don't think you fit that type. I'm sorry, I don't intend to be mean or anything. I just know what I want and I'm going to do all I can to get it."

That stunned Liam. He mumbled, "Okay, I'll see you around then. My offer still stands if you ever change your mind."

"Thanks, but I doubt it."

A serious put-down. Come to think of it, he

didn't even have any idea what he wanted to do after high school. He grew confused and angry. He watched her cute little butt walk away, her short skirt swaying from side to side. His eyes burned and his nostrils flared. So, he headed for the gym and hit the weights like never before. Conor noticed. That day, Liam's new goal would define who he would become for his remaining months in high school, maybe for the rest of his life. For now, he would be the biggest, strongest kid in school, where even the football jocks would be in awe and fear him. If they only knew.

# 3

May 1, 1978

Now a senior with driver's education behind him, he needed to find a job so he could afford an old car, insurance and gas. He'd need pocket money to get a girl, *any* girl. By this time, both he and Conor had bulked out. The two of them were inseparable.

Jocks talk. Like they thought he and Conor were queer. Sean McKeau was an offensive lineman at six-four. Weighed a solid two-thirty-five. He and three of his large teammates approached the machines where Conor and Liam worked out. Sean sneered. "Well, looky here. The two boyfriends are playing with each other—again. So, are you two a couple?"

Liam interrupted his two-hundred-pound bench press routine. He knew he lifted heavy, but he also knew it was the number of reps—repetitions—that built corded muscle. Conor helped him place the barbell in the rack above his sculpted chest. Slick with sweat, and pounding inside from a smoldering anger that had been brewing for years, blood coursed through his veins. This was his chance to spank these jocks once and for all. He walked right up to Sean, who was a couple inches taller, but Liam's build was more defined and muscular. With no warning at all, Liam grabbed Sean's balls with his left hand, squeezed, and twisted. When Sean bent over, an overhand right hammered down onto Sean's left cheek. That blow preceded a vicious left uppercut that snapped Sean's head back. Liam then peppered his body with a couple of spleen shots to his left side and a couple more gut-pounders. He'd practiced these combinations. A lot. Sounded like someone pounding a heavy bag with a baseball bat. Sean went down and out.

Another large jock made a move to sucker punch Liam from behind. Conor saw it coming, blocked it and tagged him with a brutal blow to the temple. Put him down, too. Conor winced and shook his hand in pain after that bone-on-bone strike, but grinned like it was Christmas morning. Sean's other two friends stood there, frozen in their tracks. Liam nodded his thanks to Conor and said, "Next?" Nothing. "No? Then how 'bout you pick up these pieces a shit and get 'em the fuck outta here? From now on, if *any* a you make *any* kinda remark about me or Conor ever again, we'll put you runts down just like these assholes. Nod if you understand me." Liam growled and sneered to emphasize the gravity of his command. The two nodded, helped their friends up, and off they stumbled. Word got out. Nobody messed with Conor and Liam, or said a word about them from that day forward. They continued their friendship and their bodybuilding. If they could see their future, however, they'd ride a different road. They could not.

# 4

June 13, 1979

Karamusell, Pennsylvania

Nobody ever accused Liam Sullivan of being handsome, only feared. Now, more than a year downrange of high school, Liam sought some sort of purpose. But tonight, they cruised in his old 1972 Chevy C10 pickup whose most predominant feature was premature rust. Through his passenger's side window on a dim and almost deserted street, Liam's friend, Conor, spotted Ginny Swanson—little *Miss Perfect*—walking with a tall, lanky guy as they passed under a streetlight. "Liam, check it out." Liam rolled to a stop with softly squealing brakes.

Conor rolled down the window. "Hi Ginny. Remember us? Want a ride?"

Skinny said, "No thanks. We're good." They kept walking. Ginny remained silent, but kept peering over her shoulder with squinted eyes. Their pace quickened. She clutched Skinny's arm tighter with both of hers.

Liam pasted on a grin that displayed his crooked, yellow teeth. It was the smile of a lonely young man from the wrong side of nowhere. He yelled across Conor's chest. "Aw, c'mon Ginny. Let's party tonight." He didn't mean his words to sound like pleading, but they did.

Skinny shouted in a shaky voice without making eye contact—looking straight ahead, "We're not looking for a ride, *or* any trouble. Please leave us alone."

Liam remembered the put-down Ginny dropped on him a year earlier in high school. He jammed the truck's shift lever on the steering column up into *Park*, jumped out, and stumbled. A solitary empty beer can clattered to the asphalt. After recovering from his misstep, he looked back at the street as if to spot a nonexistent object in the street that had caused him to trip. He shuffled up to Skinny with

Ginny now begging Liam with her eyes to leave them alone. Liam blocked their path, still trying to smile, but only succeeded in baring his poor-side-of-town overbite. Didn't know what to do with his arms and hands as he looked at her. They hung at his side, useless appendages. He leaned toward her. She leaned away. Still got close enough to smell her hair—like... lilacs?

She'd filled out since last year when she was already a knockout. Then, Liam did what came natural to him. One punch to Skinny's stomach, an overhand right to the head, and the bone bag went down, face up on the sidewalk, head and upper torso over the curb and into the street. Ginny jumped back, frozen in shock three feet away. Liam flipped Skinny over and dug an old wallet out of his right-rear jeans pocket. Forty-two dollars in bills. "A lot of cash to be carrying around, dude. Your loss."

As he squatted by Ginny's unconscious date, he thought he succeeded in not slurring his words. He failed. Stuffed the cash in his own front pocket. Liam stood up, turned and advanced on Ginny. Grabbed her by her shoulders. She squealed, "You're hurting me!"

Now, seeing what was happening, Conor jumped out of the truck with an old roll of duct tape he'd retrieved from behind the seat. Tore off a six-inch hunk and slapped it over Ginny's mouth as gently as he dared. He tried not to look at her eyes locked wide-open in shock and surprise.

"Conor, grab her legs." Liam grabbed her under her arms, and they tossed her onto the truck's tailgate sideways where Conor taped her hands, Liam her legs. Rolled her farther in and slammed the tailgate. They left Skinny lying face down in the gutter, still unconscious. Conor looked at Liam. His eyes asked, *Now what?* Liam said nothing, but his body language signaled he had a plan for where they'd go next, and why.

---

They drove down a rutted blacktop road, then gravel. The back of Ginny's head bounced off the pickup's rusty steel bed beneath her. Everything hurt. Overwhelming fear made everything worse. Even breathing hurt and came hard. Felt her stomach cramp. After a long while, she felt the truck slow down as the ride grew smoother. Realized they'd pulled off the road onto a grassy trail. She could smell... forest? Stopped near a secluded patch of woods. She watched Liam slam open the tailgate. Couldn't see the road. They dragged her from the pickup's corrugated bed. Her head bounced. She dreaded the best outcome—that they'd "only" rape her. But would they then kill her? Tears streamed down her face. They cut the tape that bound her legs, but did not free her hands or mouth. Liam was the roughest.

The hours dragged by. Ginny's pain graduated to a numb nightmare. These two drunken boys—these monsters—ravaged her so many times she lost count. For some reason, she tried to keep count. Imagined that might be useful in a court of law if she survived. But she lost count. Then, she merely wished she were dead. She felt dead already, even before she blacked out.

In a delirious fit of passion, Liam sliced off a fistful of Ginny Swanson's hair, right up top, with the razor-sharp hunting knife he always kept nearby, even when his pants were down around his ankles. But he cut right down into her scalp. It bled. *Oh, man, that's gotta hurt.* Didn't mean to cut that close. Just happened. But he liked it. Tucked the lock of hair away after sniffing it a few times. Made him hot. No idea why. She tried to scream, but the ultra-sticky tape over her mouth only allowed an explosive dribble of mucus and watery blood from both flaring nostrils. She followed that muffled scream with a squeaky moan. Even *that* he found erotic. Ginny was his first. Well, sort of.

Way too much tape around her wrists prevented her from clutching at her now-bleeding scalp. Not sure if she was bawling, shivering, or both. *So cold on these wet leaves. Dark, too.* The only light shot out into the woods from the still-burning pickup's headlights. They pointed off to Liam's left, to the edge of their small clearing. *We shoulda spread a blanket first. Oh, well.* He finished again. Wiped thick saliva from his mouth onto the forearm of his jean jacket sleeve. Thirsty. Got to his knees. Pulled up his damp Levi's and shivered. Conor's turn.

They'd left Ginny's scrawny date—what was his name?—lying bloody on the sidewalk with his head face down in the gutter a block from her parent's house hours earlier now, and twenty miles away. She'd been on his mind ever since that high school thing, especially after they both graduated the previous summer.

Conor's turn—did he look scared? Not too scared for another round. The sun threatened to pop up over the trees anytime now. Liam stumbled over to the truck to shove the headlight switch in to save the battery—what was left of it, anyway.

. . .

When Liam and Conor sated themselves hours later and sobered up, they realized they needed to think beyond their next erection. Liam still liked Ginny, but now she was damaged goods. He'd need to decide whether to finish her off when they were done and leave her body with her shredded clothes now scattered around her. *We shoulda thought ahead! But we ain't no killers.*

"What do we do with her now?" Conor asked.

"Got no stomach for killin' someone I like."

"Me neither, Liam. Not sure about killin' nobody."

"Yeah, me too. Shit!"

Conor had built a small fire some time after they arrived while Liam was busy with Ginny. That fire now burned down to gray ash, even after throwing some more dried sticks he'd found at the edge of their small clearing awhile back. Conor worried about Ginny losing and regaining consciousness. A lot. *Maybe she's just pretending. Yeah, that's gotta be it.*

Now, the boys hunched over the fire's few remaining embers glowing from within a coat of white ash. Ginny now sprawled on the old blanket they'd carried around in the truck for a long time. Stunk like oil and old garage. She was far enough away from them and the fire that they were sure she couldn't overhear their now headache-plagued whispers. Liam said, "I'll handle this." He approached Ginny, her hands and mouth still taped, and barely conscious. She shivered like it might be her last one. Liam saw goose bumps where there wasn't any blood or other stuff. Her eyes fluttered open. Pulled away from his touch. He muttered, "I'm sorry, Ginny. This sorta got outta control. Don't know what else to say." Conor had followed him over, watching and listening. Liam turned and said, "Cut the tape and leave her the blanket. We gotta go,"

"*Leave her?* But when she gets back to Karamusell, she's goin' to the cops. And then we're in for it."

"Yeah, I know. But how 'bout we beat feet and get the hell outta this state? We'll pack our shit up from the apartment and hit the road."

"Great idea, Liam. No money to get anywhere and nothin' to live on? We're screwed, you know that, right?"

"I know. But for now, let's see how it plays out. We'll pick up our last paychecks and start drivin'. We might catch a break."

Liam cut Ginny loose. Looked like she'd cry if she had any tears left. He covered her with the blanket, now sticky and wet as hell. "Make it out to the road and you'll be okay, Ginny."

It took until late the next day to get their last paychecks. They became more and more agitated at the delay. With the truck gassed up, they headed north-northeast on Route 209 toward New England. They made decent time once they finally hit the road even though they avoided the interstate. Their only goal: to get the hell out of Pennsylvania. They didn't talk much. Liam thought, *How did things get so out of control so fast?*

Knowing they'd never return, Karamusell was already little more than a bad memory. Or so they thought.

# 5

Two hours later, Ginny wandered out of the woods to the road and was found. She identified her attackers. Every police department and the Pennsylvania Highway Patrol had received state-wide alerts: *All-Points Bulletin* and *Be On the Look Out*. Their target was Liam Sullivan's truck. The APB and BOLO described its occupants from their driver's licenses and the truck's description from its registration.

An hour after receiving the alerts, veteran Pennsylvania State Police Trooper Lloyd Kreutch sat in his cruiser behind a roadside billboard forty miles north-northeast of Karamusell. On Route 209, he spotted the nineteen-seventy-two Chevy C10 pickup —more rust than brown—occupied by two individuals. It cruised by him at twenty-four miles per hour over the posted speed limit of sixty. The BOLO warned the occupants were potentially armed and dangerous.

Trooper Kreutch called it in, lit up, and peeled out to pursue. The pickup did not try to accelerate or escape. It just pulled over to the side of the road in the breakdown lane. Kreutch hated bullies, and worse, sex offenders. After stopping the vehicle with his weapon drawn and aimed at the back of the driver's head, Trooper Kreutch took two muscular young men into custody without incident. Back-up arrived and his apprehension subsided. These were two young bruisers. He remanded them to the Karamusell County Jail to be held without bail pending trial. They were accused of assaulting a young man and raping his girlfriend. *Hope these assholes get what they deserve.*

---

Liam and Conor were then in the system. Ginny remained in the hospital for three agonizing days and nights as she had succumbed to both emotional and physical exhaustion from exposure and acute trauma. They kept her medicated to allow the wounds and stitches to heal. She'd likely need a small skin graft to her scalp. Even then, hair might never grow back in that spot, they told her.

The trial took place two months later. They charged the two men together with kidnapping, aggravated rape, two counts of aggravated assault, and a single count of unarmed robbery. Liam and Conor expressed sorrow and regret with sincere apologies. Being first-time offenders, they did not levy the maximum penalty allowed. The six-man, six-woman jury took less than two hours to render a guilty verdict on all five counts for both men. They were only sentenced to ten years in the state prison at Albion, Pennsylvania. Hard time within a hard-core population. They'd made the big leagues less than a year out of high school.

The boys found life in prison better than working in the mills, but struggled with the regimentation, crappy food, and day-to-day life under constant threat. The gangs presented the greatest danger. They did not fit in with the Crips, Bloods, or Arians, so they watched each other's backs. Their size and rough demeanor served them well here, but *the life* only bred more resentment towards *society*. They managed to stay out of solitary, but spent every free moment with weights and workouts. Other convicts were huge and made them feel small. One giant black con named Lakeith looked at them and said, "My *shadow* could kick your runt asses."

Their new goal? To be as big, if not bigger, than any of the other cons, but also to maintain agility. The boys realized muscles were fine, but they also needed quickness and flexibility to prevail in a brawl. They were in the right place to learn about survival of the fittest. Both witnessed and fell prey to every dirty fighting trick by getting their asses kicked on a regular basis. But the boys learned from it all. The days, months, and years dragged by for Liam and Conor, as they grew more grizzled and more mean.

---

Now, as the end of their ten-year sentence drew near, they faced their slim prospects *outside* as hardened convicts with multiple felony convictions.

They'd be unemployable. So, Liam and Conor obtained their freedom, but were not free.

Feeling even more sexually oppressed, they continued to blame *society* for their plight, whoever that included. They swore a renewed allegiance to one another. At thirty, they now had to make a new life for themselves. Somehow.

# 6

May 20, 1988
Framingham, Massachusetts

M

Sam Travis hadn't visited the Massachusetts Environmental Police Academy a half-hour west of Boston in years. But he was ordered to appear. He knew by whom and why. The academy's commandant and he needed to finish something together. Trust didn't come easy these days, not even within law enforcement. So they treated this like an off-the-books operation. Both knew how to do that all too well. But their unfinished business had nothing to do with the academy.

Travis hadn't forgotten this place: the painted

brick buildings, the sense of excitement and antici-pation in the air... so thick he could almost smell it. If it hadn't been for the discipline this place instilled in him, his life might have gone in a very different direction. Not a good one. A gilded sign of gold, black, and green, with white letters near the facili-ty's entrance gate and guardhouse announced this was a military-style installation:

> ### Environmental Police Academy
> ### Framingham, Massachusetts

Some of the old-fashioned buildings on the campus looked even more old-fashioned with pillars and porches. Groups of cadets marched with drill instructors counting cadence. Memories—mostly pleasant—flooded Sam's mind at the sights and sounds. How long had it been since he was a cadet? He felt as old as some of these structures. He'd dragged his mind and body down some hard roads since then. Approached an ordinary door on the main floor of the administration building. The sign on the door read:

> Captain L. Jamison,
> Academy Commandant

Sam knocked and entered the outer office. His smile was a mask to cover what was going on inside. What was his secretary's name? He pretended he remembered until he got close enough to read the name plate on her desk. "Ellie, so good to see you again. Remember me?"

Ellie blushed. She had passed her prime a decade earlier, but she was still a beautiful woman *and* a force of nature. "Officer Travis, it's good to see you, too."

"I'd come around more often, but I'd hate to make your husband jealous." He winked.

Ellie's blush blossomed even as she smirked. "Like you have a shot, young man."

They both chuckled. As expected. She said, "Go right in," and she winked back at him. He shook his head from side to side. Too much woman for him, anyway.


One quick knock later, Sam swung open the door to Jamison's office. "Sir." Neither man smiled. They were about to discuss how they might bring down a corrupt federal agent from the US Fish and Wildlife Service, or USFWS—a fed—and likely another high-level conspirator or two in the bargain, maybe within their own organization, as well. Sam would do whatever it took to both disguise the venomous hatred he nurtured for both of these criminals, *and* to go to any lengths to see these dirtbags in prison, or preferably, in the ground. He ensured his neutral mask did not crack.

"Sit, Sam. Let's get right to it. How the hell did Mason slip away?"

Captain Jamison—Larry—referred to Agent Kim Mason, a mid-level undercover operative—a UC—for the US Fish and Wildlife Service, or USFWS. Earlier the previous autumn, they had caught the man in deep guilty. Mason ran an illegal international wildlife trafficking ring raking in a ton of cash—millions. A trio of poachers who worked for Mason had killed Sam's partner and friend, Sergeant Frank Murdock. They'd almost killed him and Jamison, too, after kidnapping Sam's twelve-year-old son *and* beating up his girlfriend. The man was a monster—as clever as he was insidious. But someone dealt Mason a get-out-of-jail card after Sam and his boss apprehended him. Neither he nor Larry would let that stand. At least Larry seemed to control his anger over this outrage better than Sam.

"Boss, do you think Assistant U.S. Attorney Lowry is part of this? I don't know any Department of Justice employees who dress that well. And what about our own Commissioner Verdi? Do you trust him, Larry?"

"Whoa, there, Sam. That's a couple of heavy bags to be punching. But let's not eliminate any possibilities. We follow the evidence."

"And we get to keep our jobs, right?"

"How it's supposed to be. Yeah, that's the plan."

"Ideas?"

"It's always the money... we follow the money."

Sam piped up with an exasperated edge to his voice. "But how do we do that, boss?"

Larry scratched his chin. He fell silent for almost a minute. Their situation seemed impossible. These two state cops were squaring off against some heavy hitters—a federal law enforcement officer *and* an assistant US Attorney within the Department of frickin' Justice. Both feds, and neither one of them dummies. Plus, maybe their own commissioner as well.

Sam waited. Then he said, "Hey, I know a guy who knows money."

"You trust him? With our jobs? Our lives, even?"

"Let's find out." Sam's smirk did not inspire confidence.

# 7

It didn't appear 1988 would be a whole lot more promising than almost ten years earlier, before a jury sent them to prison in Albion, Pennsylvania for assault and aggravated rape. But a fresh start meant a fresh start. Even got out a few months early. Liam Sullivan nodded over his left shoulder as they slumped out of the prison's gates. "Hey, Conor, not sure 'bout you, but I'm done with PA. Place sucks. What about New England? Maybe Maine?

Conor didn't imagine they'd do any better in a strange state. "Sure, Liam. Why not, right? Who's gonna stop us?" Striking out on his own without Liam never occurred to him.

"There ya go. Let's do it. We can pick up jobs. Maybe pump gas to pay the rent, buy food and some new clothes."

Conor kept wondering, though. *At least nobody knows us in Maine.*

So, off they trudged, after retrieving Liam's rusty old Chevy pickup from his mom's garage. Conor's truck was sold at auction soon after he went to Albion. Liam's dad? Long-gone. *A good thing for Liam's Mom.* His little brother Mac was gone, too. Not sure where.

---

Liam and Conor saw themselves as new men full of possibilities. After some frivolous and reckless first-night-out fun a hundred miles north of Karamusell, they passed a sign late the next day announcing they'd arrived in Blue Hill, Maine after driving for nine hours, population: 1,934 souls. Spotted a cardboard sign alongside an intersection:

*Help wanted.*
*No references or*
*background checks required.*
*Start right away.*
*See Mel at*
*Hammond Lumber*

*Bingo.* Mel, the boss at Hammond, took one gander at them and said, "Let's get you to work jackin' lumber, boys. Start ya at fifteen an hour. You last a month, we bump ya to eighteen. At six months, twenty." He turned and led the way to a four-axle truck.

The boys thought they'd died and gone to heaven. They started out bucking up fallen trees—removing limbs. Brute fast-paced work for which they seemed well-suited. Liam graduated to cutting down trees, and attaching cables to logs for transport. He possessed a knack. Conor? Not so much. But they worked the same shifts on the same crew.

Jacking lumber kept them in shape. They liked the food and the job included free room and board. They found a new comfort in the woods performing mindless tasks, although Liam needed his wits about him to fell trees. Conor remained on the crew cutting and bucking up hemlock, pine, and old stands of red oak in the vast forests that surrounded Blue Hill. It suited him.

But they both felt something was missing. Even the trips into town, the bars, the shack-ups? All unsatisfying. They craved something. Not sure what —an itch that needed scratching in the worst possible way.

# 8

After a month on the job, Mel at Hammond Lumber bumped their pay—as promised—and moved them to another logging camp that came close to intercepting something called the Appalachian Trail. Locals called it *the AT*. It astounded both Liam and Conor watching the trail's hikers with all their expensive gear. What possessed these granola-munching tree-huggers to *walk* over two thousand miles—*for the fun of it?* Rich assholes with too much time and money on their hands. They found the entire concept so inconceivable that it caused rage to bubble up from somewhere deep inside Liam first, then Conor.

In this small town of Rangely, Maine, near a trail

access point, the boys slouched at the end of the joint's tiny bar. Nothing more than a local barroom that catered first to locals, but also to a few of the more adventurous hikers taking a break. Several of them seemed to hike alone. And not just men. Women, too. Some alone, some downright attractive, and most in top physical shape.

Liam hunkered at that bar shoulder-to-shoulder with Conor. He kept his voice low. "Hey Con, in them deep forests, what if ya screamed your fool lungs out with nobody to rescue ya? Wonder what it would be like to hunt us one a them hiker babes over there?" He nodded toward a couple of attractive young women all geared up with huge packs leaning against the wall on the floor behind them. "But way away from the work site, a course." He swiveled his downcast gaze from his beer bottle to glance sideways into Conor's lowered eyes. Conor thought Liam was just talking trash and snorted at the proposition, but one look into his old friend's slitted eyes? He grew deadly serious.

Liam scratched the stubble on his neck that threatened to sprout into a beard as he continued, now with a brittle edge to his gravelly whisper. More guttural. "Yeah, take us a little revenge. That's owed to us, man. Thin out this here snooty hiker herd by one or two. After some fun, a course. Who the hell'd know? We learned some good stuff in the pen. 'Member that guy Lakeith who done all them boys? Woulda never got nailed 'cept his whore ratted him out. He was smart about DNA, weapons, body dumps... all that sciency shit. Now, *we* got what he done taught us, Conor. We can do this, an' get us a little sweet payback."

"Dunno, Liam. I *can't* go back to the pen, man."

Liam's voice remained a throaty whisper, but cold as polished steel on ice. "So we don't get caught. Our mistake? We left that little slut Ginny too close to a road. Man, we got this. A couple a knives, a tent, some rain gear, and we are good to go, man. We'd need a trial run, a course. See how that goes."

A slow grin crept across Conor's face. Yup, they'd make a plan. That night in their tiny company cabin, they sat on Liam's bunk, conspiring in whispers so the other two jacks in their bunks couldn't hear. The pot-belly wood-burner crackled when they started. But those embers died and turned to ash by the time they'd talked out their plan. Liam said, "The mountains snatch another stupid hiker or two. Who's to say *why* they disappear?"

"Hell, yeah. Let's get us some, partner."

That night, or what was left of it, they slept like babies, content for the first time in over a decade.

They'd take a couple of days off. Road trip the next day after work. Boss'd understand a few days gone. After all, Mel *needed* Liam and Conor on the crew. And if he objected, well, that'd be alright, too.

Next night at the same bar, "Here's to fresh starts, partner." Liam clinked Conor's beer glass with his own.

Conor had his doubts, but said nothing. He'd regret that soon enough.

# 9

Tyringham, Massachusetts
June 19, 1988

---

Still at home munching on a bagel with a schmear, Sam snatched the phone off the wall on its second ring. While he and Larry Jamison, Captain and EPO Academy Commandant, ran their side-hustle for their unfinished affair—that would take awhile—Larry implored Sam to brief a recent academy graduate. This kid was one of Larry's mentees, and a potential replacement for Sam's deceased partner, Sergeant Frank Murdock. So far, they hadn't had any luck replacing Frank. Larry said he was keeping his eye on the kid. A ride-along is all, he said. Sam's immediate boss, Lieutenant Paul O'Neill, weighed in on the assignment. He was in Larry's office with him at the academy for the call. LT polished Sam's apple, saying he was now a veteran EPO with a great deal of field wisdom to offer. The kids's name was Officer Allen Stukowski. He'd even drive to Sam's office in Glenville to meet him.

An hour later. Stukowski approached him before Sam even slid out of his Bronco. Eager, of course. Cadets often were. "So, Officer Stukowski, what kind of name is that?"

"Polish, sir. Second generation. Parents thought Allen was a real good American name for a real American. That's me."

Sam rolled his eyes, but smiled. "Okay, Allen, let's go." The kid hopped into the passenger's side of Sam's olive green Bronco, his official EPO cruiser. He seemed a little too eager. He'd do okay. "Listen, Allen, don't hurry to be a superstar out here. It takes time—*should* take time."

"What do you mean, sir?"

"How 'bout you stow that sir crap, Al. Sam or Travis will do."

"Yes, sir... Sam. Nobody's ever called me Al before."

"Gonna be a day of firsts for you, Al. When you're new in any assignment to a new region, most say it takes years to learn every nook and cranny in that district. Just the nature of this job. So there's a lot of driving down roads to see where they connect. Logging roads are often tricky to navigate, but they provide remote access we need as EPOs. So, pick a town in our district and learn every road, back road, dead end, and alley. Focus first on areas where folks are likely to be breaking laws. Develop a good relationship with the local cops. They have a lot to offer. We call time spent on this important part of the job in our daily reports *area familiarization*.

"Likewise, there'll be individuals who approach you and offer information—tips—just to see how you'll react and what you'll do. A lot of that is bullshit. But every once in a while, someone will give you good actionable info. Then, it's a lot of surveillance to determine whether any of those tips are righteous or raw baloney. Never know where something like that'll pay off.

"Such a complaint came in from a young man about your age I had met while teaching a firearms safety class. Got a name and a location where a repeated violation had been taking place; no names, just a general description. This decent, well-spoken guy suspected the offender he described was poaching stocked fish that other fishermen could be catching legally. So, I developed a source to discover actionable intel."

"Intel?"

"Good gawd, man, what else didn't they teach you at the academy? Intel, short for intelligence, or information you learn and act on to catch a bad guy. Anyway, this pond resembled a bowl in shape. At the top of the bowl was a state boat ramp. At the bottom of the bowl was a causeway. The Department of Fisheries and Wildlife, a separate agency from us Environmental Police, if you didn't know, had stocked beautiful rainbow, brown, and sometimes brook trout in that pond. Brook trout have a higher temperature tolerance. The rainbows are most susceptible to warmer water. So it's a 'put and take' proposition. Got it?"

The kid scratched his head and muttered, "Listen to what people tell you, filter out the crapola, bad guy catching a lot of nice fish illegally after Fisheries planted them, but we need more intel to prosecute. Like that? Sam?" Al smiled big. He knew he was right.

*Okay, the kid's sharper than he lets on. Might make a good UC some day. Not everybody can handle an undercover gig.* They had driven most of the streets of

Glenville, a small village, and now prowled the surrounding country mountain roads.

"Keep your eyes open out here, Al. Pay attention to where you are at all times—signs like mile markers, major visual landmarks, even the type of road you're on. We call that situational awareness—in case you spot something and gotta call in your location, or God forbid, call for backup.

"Anyway, I learned my target's name was Taxi Fairchild. I thought it was a nickname. Who names their kid *Taxi*, right? He was past middle age, average height and weight, and was one hell of an angler. He'd catch more than most, and more frequently. Fished alone. Suspicious of people fishing next to him—he'd get in his car and move off. Not sociable, at least not when wetting a line. He bragged in the local barrooms that no warden was smart enough to catch him. Well, that's like putting me on the starting block at a track meet, waiting for the gun to go off.

"Binoculars are an EPO's best friend, Al. I spied on Taxi from the boat ramp while he fished this causeway." Sam nodded toward the bridge off to their right that crossed over the point at which a couple-acre patch of smooth water burbled from a stream at the south end. "Earlier, I had ditched my cruiser in that copse of trees over there, just out of sight of the causeway, because a green marked car is an easy spot, even from a distance. So, with my trusty binos, I watched. And then watched some more. In less than an hour, I saw him stash a stocked fish into his trunk three times before he took off.

"I called Fish and Wildlife to ask what other lakes were being stocked that day. They informed me another was Leisure Lake a few miles away, which also has a causeway opposite a boat ramp. Guess who showed up at the causeway's bridge *after* having caught his daily bag limit? Yup, Taxi. I made his car and set up another hide. Taxi caught more trout. Again. But the clever old boy used a trick stringer. Know what a stringer is, Al?"

The kid looked at Sam like he'd been insulted. "Uh, *yeah*. A line used to attach fish and keep them in the water and alive rather than sit in a cooler in a hot trunk."

"Very good, kid. But here's a twist you might not know about. Taxi was clever. He installed a break-away so that if approached, one flick of a finger and the fish on his stringer hanging in the water swam away. No evidence. Getting to that stringer before he'd release his illegal catch seemed difficult, if not impossible. How could I approach so as not to spook him into activating his breakaway?"

They had driven to Leisure Lake to provide the

kid a visual context of Sam's *UC 101* lecture. He felt like a damn professor, but secretly admitted he relished reliving a memorable story for this eager former cadet. "So what the hell did you do, Sam?" The first profanity he'd heard out of this clean-cut kid's mouth. Sounded out of place. Sam smirked. Al was fitting in. Good.

"Well, I checked out several joggers on the trail around the lake. Old Taxi didn't pay them any attention as they passed by on the causeway and kept going. Okay, jogging it is. No uniform, hidden badge, firearm, and handcuffs. I let him fish for about an hour. Then, I made my move in sunglasses, baseball cap, sneakers and running pants. I keep that shit in the Bronc in my UC bag, along with a few other goodies. Anyway, I ran by him and nodded. He fidgeted. Didn't nod back. I jogged to the rise over there on the far side of the causeway, hid in the bushes and watched. More fish into the cooler in the trunk—not using his trick stringer. That meant he wasn't sticking around for long. So, I jogged back toward his car. Timed it so I got there just as he opened his trunk. I started a conversation he didn't want to have. I needed to spring my trap.

"In a loud voice, making it as intimidating as possible to keep him off balance and compliant, I *shouted* while shoving my badge in his face. I gave him a gander at my firearm sticking out of my jogging pants. 'State Environmental Police, forthwith display all fish, birds or mammals in your possession.' I saw he was visibly shaken. He had a blank, confused look on his face. I then mirandized him. Cite the words back to me, Al."

"Um, 'you have the right to remain silent. Anything you say can and will be used in a court of law. You have the right to an attorney before any questioning. If you cannot afford an attorney, one will be appointed to you by the Commonwealth of Massachusetts. Do you understand your rights as I have explained them to you?'"

"Very good, Al. I got a nod from old Taxi. I said to him, 'I must have an answer.'

"He said, 'yes.' In a softer voice, I added, 'Sir, are you armed in any way? I'm going to search you for our protection.' Taxi shook his head. It can be unnerving for your detainee. You're spinning him around, and putting your hands on a person is invasive, but permissible. I patted the old boy down. Clean. I said to him, 'Get those fish out of your trunk and put them on the ground.' Five trout. Two over the limit.

"He was shaking and asked, 'Am I under arrest?'

"'I haven't decided yet. You could be facing jail time.' Now he was *really* shaken.

"He almost whined, 'No, please! No jail. I can't do jail. Is there another way?'

"Now Al, this is how you develop a CI—a confidential informant. I said, 'Well, I could cite you non-criminally, seize your fish and equipment until you pay the fines.' He jumped at *my* bait.

"'Please, officer, I'll do anything.' Now I knew he'd make a useful local snitch. Taxi knew *everybody* —good and bad. So be it. I passed him a handful of citations, took his gear and his fish. Now, I didn't have to say what I said next, but it felt damn good. 'Do you plan on spreading the word that you can't be caught anymore?'

"He *was* whining then, 'No, no, no!'

"I added, 'You're easy pickings, Taxi. I can get you anytime I want to spend the time.' The pitiful tone in his voice told me I had him. He said, 'I'll help you any way I can. I can be useful.'

"'We'll see about that. But I expect it.'

"Taxi paid his fines, avoided arrest and turned out to be a great informant. A bonus? He let it be known that 'Travis is a good guy and a great officer.' Heard it through the grapevine. I came to like ole Taxi and he respected me. Over the years, he provided me with a few good tips that resulted in prosecutable cases, and no one was the wiser."

"Jeez, Sam, that's a great story."

"Not a story, kid. This is your first peek into the not-so-glamorous world of how a real-world undercover example produced results through developing an informant. The gift that keeps on giving."

The next day, Sam would experience another gift that keeps on giving, only not the kind he liked. At all.

# 10

Officer Al Stukowski was off to his new duty post over in Cheshire the next day. Travis gave the kid high marks, but told Lieutenant O'Neill and Captain Jamison he needed a more seasoned replacement for his deceased partner. Sam cruised his olive-drab Bronco down Beech Road near Lower Goose Pond. Margie's silky voice poured out of the dash radio's speaker like warm honey from a hot spoon. "Dispatch to Twenty-three."

"Twenty-three is on. Go ahead."

"See a Mister Perry Bismuth at 19 Brookway Hollow up in Fayville, near Beartown State Forest. A bear is displaying aggressive behavior near their rental cabin. Says he fears for his family's safety."

"Roger, dispatch. Will do." *Rich vacationers.* The Bronco jumped forward at his command. His leisurely drive home after his scheduled shift now became an urgent lives-at-risk call.

When Sam arrived ten minutes later, the "cabin" looked like a small mansion made of logs. And there was a man, a woman, and two teen-age kids—a boy and a girl—huddled together in the front yard near the road. He slid out of his Bronco, left the door open. Walked over to the family with the heel of his right hand resting on his holstered revolver. He'd already unsnapped its retainer strap. The family looked like they were cowering from a terrorist threat. With his head on a swivel, Sam said, "Where's the animal, folks?" All four pointed at the house at the same time. Sam jutted his jaw forward and cocked his head to one side. Hands now on his hips, he said, "Were you folks feeding the bear?" His steely gaze was unambiguous and broadcast, *Don't you dare lie to me.*

The father looked sheepish. "Only tossed part of a PBJ sandwich at him, is all. But from a safe distance out here in the yard. Then, he wouldn't go away."

"'Safe distance?' And you'd know what that is? Sir, didn't you read the 'Do Not Feed the Wildlife' signs posted everywhere, including right out in front of your house, here?" Sam pointed to the sign at the curb not twenty feet from where they stood. "He or she wanted more. Now until October, these bears eat like pigs to prepare for hibernation. Natural instinct. What happened next?"

"We went inside and locked the door. Heard it scratching. So we called you. But then a minute later a lot of noise came from the kitchen. The damn thing tore the air conditioner unit right out of the mudroom window and climbed in! We ran back out the front door and closed it. Not sure how he fit through that small window."

"Sir, a hundred-seventy-five-pound black bear will fit anywhere a man fits. You feed these wild animals, they'll just keep coming back for more. Easy pickings for them. This used to be virgin forest not that long ago. They'll continue seeking food by spending the least amount of energy. You're enabling that. And a window won't stop them. Now, unfortunately, I may have to put it down. Depends if the bear is what we call a *repeat offender*. Did you see any yellow or red paint on the bear?"

The man's wife squealed and punched her husband in the shoulder. With her teeth bared. She looked downright feral and spoke in a mocking tone. "Now look what you've done, Perry! 'Only a part of a peanut butter sandwich,' you said—"

"And jelly—"

"Perry, shut up! Officer, we feel awful about this, but will you get that poor animal out of our kitchen now, please?"

Sam had to get them focused. "Did you spot any yellow or red paint on the bear's rear quarters?"

The woman screeched, *"What?"*

"Ma'am, before killing an aggressive animal, we get their attention with a bean bag round from a shotgun. Hurts like the blazes, but is non-lethal. The first time, the bag deploys a large spot of permanent yellow paint. The second *offense* we hit 'em with red paint. After that...."

The boy said, "I saw a splotch of yellow paint, sir."

Now rattled and not smart enough to keep his mouth shut, the man muttered, "Can't you take him to a zoo or something?" It embarrassed him, this turn of events. That was clear.

"Not that simple, sir. Most zoos are on a budget. And most already have black bears. Once a bear learns aggressive behavior, there are few alternatives." He patted his hip holster to emphasize the last resort. Too bad if they felt shitty. *They should, damn it.*

One of the teenagers piped up. "Can't you just tranquilize the poor thing?"

"Not like the movies, young lady. Tranqs shock a bear's system. When they're released, they may come to, walk off, but about half the time they die. They don't show that on TV, do they? So instead, we immobilize them with a different kind of drug. They remain fully conscious with no muscle control whatsoever, but that traumatizes them, too. We do what we can. Either way...." He gave her his best disappointed cop glare. The girl looked both shocked and embarrassed.

Sam Travis, Environmental Police Officer for the Commonwealth of Massachusetts, hated this part of his job. All because ignorant city folks ignored a sign, right in their front yard. Now, he might have to put down some cub's mama. "Folks, go get in your car and stay there. Now." The volume and firmness of Sam's voice left no doubt this was a command. The family did so with the wife still slugging her husband in the arm, and still snarling at him.

Sam opened the rear gate of his Bronco to retrieve his seven-shot pump-action twelve-gauge shotgun. He loaded the chamber with a color-coded non-lethal bean bag round that also contained a red paint pellet. If necessary, a lethal twelve-gauge slug would follow right behind it. Normally, he'd only load double-ought buckshot. But that wouldn't stop a bear, only piss it off. He hoped he wouldn't have to use the huge rifled slug—an absolutely devastating round.

As Sam approached the house's front door, he held the long barrel of the heavy gun level and ready. When scared or pissed, a black bear will move faster than most folks imagine. His plan was to open an easy path for the bear to exit without getting mauled. That meant getting behind it and staying out of its path on its way out. That was the plan, anyway.

He opened the door with caution and heard clattering noises in the kitchen. The wife had directed him to make his way to the right through the formal dining room (in a *cabin?*) and to the kitchen toward the back of the house. He'd clear that path to the open front door through the living room. After making his way to the archway between the dining room and the kitchen, though, Sam saw the lumbering bear had torn off the refrigerator door, now with her head inside. He hollered, "Hey!" knowing he was taking a risk interrupting her buffet meal.

She turned her head, startled, snarled, and lunged for him on all fours—at speed. Sam pulled the trigger, pumped, and fired again at near point-blank range. His training had kicked in. He'd instinctively drawn an imaginary line from one of her ears to the opposite eye. Then another from her other ear to its opposite eye. Where those lines intersected—an imaginary X—he'd automatically aimed and angled his shot down toward the neck. Like turning off a switch at her brain stem, the bear just dropped in mid-growl with a prolonged and noisy exhale. No pain. Sam hated this part of the job. Quivering from the high emotion of a violent and senseless kill, he retrieved the portable radio clipped to his belt tucked in the small of his back, well out of the way. He stared down at the motionless animal now at his feet. Softly into the radio, "Dispatch, busy for the next hour. Still at 19 Brookway Hollow. Loading one deceased bear onto my carry rack. I'll take her over to Harriet's Meat Locker to process for the food shelter."

"Sorry, Sam. I know how much you hate—"

He interrupted the EPO dispatcher. "Thanks, Margie. Yeah, no choice. A second offender, immediate aggression apparent."

"Copy that."

# 11

An hour later, Sam drove home to his own cabin, which was *not* a mini-log-mansion —just a story-and-a-half three-bed, two-bath cabin with an eat-in kitchen, a nice porch, a floor-to-ceiling flagstone fireplace with a one-hundred-thirty-year-old oak mantel, Sam's office with a sign on the door that read *the beatings will continue until morale improves,* and a few nice nooks in which to relax. Sam felt like crap. Plopped down on the sofa facing a pleasant fire, and tried hard not to talk about this crappy day. Kate stared at him. "Sam, I'm worried."

"About what? Tough day, is all. You know."

"No, I don't. What's going on? Something

happened, didn't it?" She'd read him like his mind was an open pamphlet on clinical depression—today, anyway.

"Killing is never easy, even when there's a good reason."

"Oh, Sam, you shot someone today."

He said nothing, at first. "I shot a bear today, Kate. She was just hungry, and these fool tourists…. Dunno. Pisses me off so bad I…." Silent and sullen, he just hung his head. *Shake it off, cowboy.*

While she was relieved he had shot no body with two legs, she saw how hard he took this. He sat there in front of the fire, crackling on a low burn in the hearth. He turned to Kate with a dour expression. Hid behind a weak smile, a flimsy mask. "Kate, don't you tire of my moods and what I do to deal with them?"

"Aw, c'mon, Sam. We share stuff. Just that some of your stuff has a little more… drama than my dull reporter stories. Unless you count the paper cut I got today." She held up her right forefinger. A quarter-inch mini-slash emphasized the rationale for her pouted lips and artificial frown.

He hoisted a still-tired smile. "Got hazard pay?"

"This is nothing. Our senior editor, George Orwell—real last name is Ondwell—thought there was an office conspiracy against him. He was convinced someone dumped a cup of water on the tile floor in front of the water cooler so *he'd* fall and break his fool neck."

"Wait. I'm a little vague on literary references, but wasn't George Orwell the guy who wrote that book, '1984?' Big Brother is watching, and all that?"

"Very good, Professor Travis. Yeah, George is always looking over his shoulder for excuses why things don't work out. A big reason why he's not a reporter in the field. That would be a stumble-down disaster. But the man *is* a decent editor."

---

Sam chuckled. This is what he needed... a distraction. But then he recalled almost dying during that last undercover op with that international poaching ring the previous Fall. "Kate, I'm serious. Doesn't it bother you hanging around a guy like me? I mean, this job brought bad guys into *this house,* got you beat up, and Brian kidnapped. I can't forgive myself for what my job has done to you guys, even though you were troopers about the whole deal. How *can* you? I mean—"

"Sam, shut the hell up. I'm not some porcelain doll to worry about. I'm a big girl. And Brian is young, strong, and you got him back. Unharmed.

We're okay. Besides, love conquers all, or did that memo get lost, *Professor?*" She reached across her body with her left arm and grabbed his chin to move in for a gentle kiss. He turned and wrapped his arms around her. They embraced but did not kiss. He dropped his forehead to meet hers. He froze. Needed to get something out. "Kate, what about this?" He waggled his finger back and forth to encompass them both.

She pulled her forehead away from his. Looked up into his eyes. "What do you mean, babe?"

"Dunno. I mean, Brian loves you as much as I do. You guys have really bonded. And you're so good for him."

"So, you're asking about me and Brian, Sam?"

"C'mon, you get it."

"No, Sam, not really." But she tossed him a life-line and smiled.

"Aw, hell, Kate, what do you think about *us?*"

She fell silent, looked up at him, then cast her eyes downward, but said nothing. Sam Travis, Environmental Police Officer and all-around tough guy, melted into that couch and thought, *Uh-oh! What have I done?*

"Sam, I love you, and you've said you love me. Are you asking me to marry you?" She slowly raised her downcast eyes to peer into his once more.

"Well, this started out to be a fishing expedition about our relationship, but—"

She placed her palm over his mouth and said, "Yes, Sam, I'll marry you."

"Hey! What's goin' on in here? You guys neckin' again? Or suckin' face?" For no good reason, both Sam and Kate jumped like he had caught them doing something wrong. Sam's thirteen-year-old son Brian sauntered into the room, stopped munching on an apple long enough to wince. The abrupt change in mood caught all three of them by surprise. They looked wide-eyed at each other. Both laughed.

Kate recovered first. "Hey, Bri, don't look so confused. Come sit between us for a sec. Something we'd like to discuss, okay?" This was maybe the only woman who his deceased wife of three years would love to see become Brian's new mom. Funny how things work out, just when they couldn't.

Now, Brian looked worried. "Hey, you guys look awfully serious right now. Am I in trouble?"

# 12

The sun shone bright late the next morning through the windows into Sam's home office. He'd recently relocated from the basement to his den adjacent to the living room. "Hey, Jeff, this is Sam Travis. How they hangin', partner?" Even though this was only a phone conversation, Sam thought he'd smile to keep it light. Besides, after a gloomy night, Kate watched him with concern from the kitchen while she made a late breakfast. Game face. She had taken a vacation day on a Tuesday—a slow news day at the Wedgewood Courier, apparently.

"Sam! Long time. You looking to refinance?"

"No, nothing like that. Buy you lunch?"

"Oh, boy. What's up?"

"I'll tell you over lunch. Deal?"

"Do I have a choice?"

They both chuckled. After the banker checked his schedule on the desktop blotter in front of him, they agreed on Beverly's Diner at one o'clock. Sam was on a budget. Besides, Jeff was a regular there. Weird for a Harvard man, but greasy food was a balm to anyone's troubled soul, right?

Two hours later, they sat across from each other in a window booth at Beverly's on Main Street in Wedgewood. Sam had already plugged a quarter into the miniature wall-mounted juke and selected *Burning For Love* by Bon Jovi, his favorite band.

"How's Kate, Sam?"

"Aw, she's great. Still works at the paper. Helluva reporter. Gets into trouble now and then digging for a story. They love her over there. She stayed home today. How's Janey?"

"Well, she passed a year ago. Cancer."

"Oh, shit, Jeff. I'm so sorry."

The poor man's face had fallen from a smile to a sad sack of gray jowls and wrinkles. He wanted to change the subject. Travis couldn't blame him.

After retrieving a hard-won grin, he said, "So,

let's order lunch before you ask your favor. That way, if I refuse, at least I get lunch out of the deal."

They both laughed to fight back the sadness now bubbling right below the surface.

---

Both their bellies were packed with two Blue Plate Specials ten minutes later. Sam hunched over his pie and coffee as the banker relished his own dessert—Beverly's killer tiramisu. "Jeff, I think we got some corruption going on and I need some real discreet help in finding a money trail."

"Whoa, Jeff. We don't do that to our clients."

"See, that's okay, since this isn't one of your clients."

"Then—"

"You have access to banking networks, right?"

Jeff's fork loaded with a sizable payload of espresso-laced sponge cake froze halfway to his no-longer-smiling mouth. The deafening silence that followed extended to ten seconds, fifteen seconds. Jeff set his fork aside and sipped his coffee. His eyes explored the depths of his almost-empty mug. Finally, the banker said, "Oh, man, you're in serious warrant territory, Sam. Even then—"

"Please tell me what you can or can't do, Jeff. I'm

fishing, so a judge won't grant us a warrant. Please. These animals killed my partner, Sergeant Frank Murdock, and they're walking free. You feel me?"

"Why not official channels, Sam? The FBI handles money laundering cases even though every bank has a designated individual that looks for and tracks suspicious transactions. And if it's a large bank with a lot of big transactions, then it's two or more personnel. You're a state cop, for God's sake. Why aren't you calling the FBI?"

"Because we don't know who to trust. Besides, the guy we're worried about is a fed, like the feebs. *At the Department of Justice.* Otherwise—"

"Oh, brother. Now you're sucking *me* into this hornet's nest? These people sound dangerous." The banker fell silent as he shoved his dessert away. Sam waited him out. Held his gaze. Then, with a soft sideways shake of his balding head, as if resigning himself to this affair, Jeff made his decision. "Look, I have an old college friend who's a finance guy at FBI headquarters in Washington. About as far from field work as possible and still work in the Bureau. They track money at the federal level. I can ask, okay? But this could take awhile."

"Jeff, I owe you."

"Yes, you do. At least one more lunch and about forty-three thousand and change at eight percent on your cabin. But what say we re-fi below six with a deal on closing costs?" After a tense five-second reset, they indulged in an uneasy chortle, together. This was no hornet's nest as Jeff suggested. This was shark-infested water in which they were both about to swim and could run deep and dangerous. Both knew it.

"Jeff, the guy we suspect is Richard Lowry. Also, we don't think there's anything up with my boss, Tom Verdi, the commissioner of our state environmental police force. But if your guy snags a look-see for a money trail there, too?"

"Oh, Sam, I hope this doesn't come back to bite me."

"On the down-low, Jeff. If you trust your guy in DC, I trust you, and you trust me. That's a nice tight loop, right?"

"Yeah, a tight loop. Like a noose around our necks?"

# 13

After Sam put down that bear two days earlier, and while he awaited intel from Jeff's FBI DC contact, it was nice to get a call about a first offender with no yellow or red paint blotches on a bear's hind. The Pittsfield Fire Department reported an enormous black bear slept peacefully thirty feet off the ground in the crotch of a gigantic oak in one of their residential neighborhoods. An old story. Humans encroach on a wildlife habitat with expensive homes, and then they expect EPOs like Sam to remove *bears* from *their ancestral home*. Sometimes, it was the job to do just that. Like today.

Sam and fellow EPO Glenn Lingvald from Dalton

met eight fire fighters at the lady's address who called it in. They all stared up at the slumbering black bear, trying their hardest not to wake it until the cavalry—they—arrived. Then, the two EPOs stood there with them. As they looked up at a mammoth four-hundred-pound black bear, he appeared oblivious of his audience far below. Glenn muttered not too loudly, "Big sum-bitch." Glenn chewed tobacco. Spit a cheek-full of worked-over juice into the grass at his feet. *Filthy habit, but Glenn's a good shit.* Sam didn't smoke *or* chew.

Sam didn't want to wake up this monster, either. Kept his voice low, too. Said to one of the boys from PFD, "Not like retrieving a cat from a tree."

The burly young firefighter looked at Travis. "Got any ideas?"

Sam said, "Yeah, we'll immobilize him. We need to get that bad boy down without injury and relocate him. Can you guys use your *big* cat-in-a-tree extraction method?" The fire fighters nodded as if they had done this before. *Yeah, right.*

"Sounds like a plan." Glenn turned to retrieve his .30-caliber tranquilizer rifle from his cruiser. Came back with the single-shot weapon. But he also clutched two darts—ballistic syringes—each with their hypodermic needle tip embedded in a little cork ball designed to prevent an accidental dosing of a powerful immobilizing—*not* tranquilizing—cocktail of dissociative anesthetics called Ketamine and Rompum. Glenn looked over at Travis and said, "five CCs of this stuff oughta do it for this big fella. Enough to knock out a small horse in ten minutes or so." He nodded down at the darts in his hand. "So one oughta do it. Pretty fast-acting. If not, I'll reload and hit him with a second dart loaded with another three CCs, but I'd rather not. Gets risky for him. And more 'n that, maybe kill 'im."

Glenn stopped far enough from the tree and circled about twenty feet to his left to offer a decent angle on the bear's hindquarters. Quietly loaded the first dart into the rifle's chamber by drawing back the gun's bolt action. Nudged in the first dart's silver body with a bright red plume on its tail after pulling the little cork ball off the needles sharp end with his teeth. He spit it out. The feathered plume provided a small drag to keep the heavy dart containing the powerful dose of bear immobilizer headed in the right direction. Said it was quite accurate within seventy-five feet, "but then ya gotta aim high and lob it in." Glenn pulled the trigger.

Sam heard a loud *snick-pfft*. Sounded more like a pneumatic toy than a gun as the compressed $CO_2$ cartridge propelled the dart. The bear lurched in its slumber in the crotch of that big oak. Sam looked up, then at Glenn. "A pretty sound sleeper, that one." *Well, that was a bit underwhelming.* "Now, we gotta figure out when Lumpy up there is immobilized, not just dozing."

"*Lumpy?*" Glenn smirked and glanced at Sam sideways, keeping one wary eye on the big dozer. Black bears, even enormous ones like *Lumpy*, will move with surprising speed if agitated. The closest fire fighter chuckled under his breath. "Yeah, well, he does look sorta lumpy curled up like that. As good a name as any."

Ten minutes later, they watched Lumpy's front right paw that had been curled up under his chin fall out of place and hung toward the ground like a limp noodle. Swung a little when it dropped, but stayed there.

Sam said, "I believe your five CC cocktail did the trick, Glenn."

"Yeah, now what? Geez. That paw is as big around as a damn dinner plate."

They chatted with the PFD captain. Confirmed the plan to deploy their ladder truck with a block and tackle to secure the bear in a rescue harness. They used such a rig in helicopter evacuations. The captain said, "We then use it to lower him to the ground with the ladder for transport. But our biggest harness might not be big enough for this monster. Might have to augment with ropes. And getting it on him is sure to be tough. We can also use a couple rope loops to connect the tackle." PFD Captain Johnstone asked, "How long we got before he wakes up? Don't want anybody getting mauled."

Glenn looked at his watch. "It's ten AM. Let's say until maybe 11:15."

"*Maybe* 11:15?"

Glenn shrugged. The captain's wide eyes squinted. He wheeled toward his guys. "Okay, let's hustle. Before this mauler wakes up with a hangover!" The PFD crew flew into action. One ran for the ladder truck parked down the block. Jumped up behind the wheel, fired up its huge diesel engine, and rolled it into position with its ass-end some forty feet from the base of the bear's tree. A couple more headed for the control panel toward the rear of the truck. Lowered four stabilizers that descended to the grassy ground from the underbody of the fifty-foot, fifty-thousand-pound, articulated vehicle.

Once steadied, one of those same fire fighters operated the ladder's controls. The other, who had a better view of the end of the ladder, gave elevation and extension hand signals to her partner. The idea was to position the high end of the ladder six feet above the bear. But they'd do so at such an angle to enable Sam and Glenn to reach the bear and get the harness on him. That was an EPO job. They'd use PFD's rigging. Another fire fighter perched at the top of the ladder above the bear to finish hooking up the tackle to the ladder's elevated end once Glenn and Sam handed it up to him. The EPOs knew how to rig the bear for minimum trauma and for safely lowering him. Captain Johnstone thought this might be a recipe for disaster, but said nothing. He was confident in his crew and in the EPOs.

Elapsed time: ten minutes.

---

It took a good fifteen minutes to hook up the bear to Sam's satisfaction. The tackle squeaked and twisted once connected and the firefighter at the top of the ladder signaled to take up the strain. The bear's position in the tree shifted. Still immobilized, his other legs came loose and dropped. The harness and its line extensions came taught. The firefighter up top signaled everything looked good. So, the end of the ladder raised. The bear came out of the tree. He hung like a half-full bag of wet cement. And the ladder bounced at half extension until the addi-tional weight—the heavy bear—hung and swung like a big-ass pendulum. They waited for the swinging to cease. With the end of the ladder lowered level with Sam and Glenn, they climbed aboard to hitch a ride down.

The PFD operator retracted and lowered the ladder. The bear came to rest on the grass near the base of the tree. After dropping to the ground, Sam immediately covered the bear's glassy eyes with a damp towel since his eyes would stay open, but he couldn't blink to keep them moist—no muscle function but still one-hundred-percent conscious and aware. A quick wrap of duct tape held the towel in place. This all took another ten minutes. After another five minutes of wrestling the harness and ropes from around the bear's huge dead-weight torso, he was free. One fire fighter muttered to no one in particular, "Just has a few cockle burrs on his coat. Kind of silvery jet-black. Very cool being this close to him, while he's asleep, that is. His breath *really stinks*, though."

Another of the PFD crew said, "Forgot to brush his teeth this morning, maybe?" Nervous chuckles all around. Sam knelt close to the bear to retrieve the dart and to swab the site with antibiotic ointment. SOP—Standard Operating Procedure. Their patient grunted in his drug-induced state. Everyone jumped back, including Sam, before getting back to work.

. . .

A local news outlet had shown up, taking pictures, but the PPD kept the obvious TV reporter—she was too damn pretty to be anything else—and her cameraman at bay. It took another five minutes to back up and position the animal control van they'd use to transport Lumpy. Trained in such a procedure, Sam took less than three more minutes to direct the firefighters how to wrestle this monster into the back of that van.

Total elapsed time since injection so far—forty-eight minutes.

With the back doors of the van swung wide, the eight burley fire fighters struggled to gather all the parts of the bear's dead weight into the van's cargo area. He filled a good portion of this three-quarter-ton panel truck. No decent way to secure him, so he lay in a giant puddle on the floor. That took another sixteen minutes. EPO Glenn Lingvald whispered to EPO Sam Travis, "I'm getting nervous about when this ole boy is gonna start comin' back around."

Total elapsed time: sixty-four minutes.

Sam said, "Can you imagine if this critter came-to while we're driving down the road? But I know you're concerned about overdosing him, too, right?" It was obvious Sam had grown nervous, too.

"Yeah, not sure what'd happen. Never immobilized a bear this big before. And looks to be an older fella, too. Should be fine, but we gotta hustle now. How far to Old Beartown Road?" That's where they'd agreed to release him. Sam and Glenn took the van. The animal control guys refused to get anywhere near that black monster, immobilized or not.

"If we hustle, less than a half-hour."

"Cuttin' it close. Let's go."

Travis drove with Lingvald riding shotgun—literally. He held his dart gun loaded with his second dart at the ready. The animal control van displayed flashing yellow caution lights on the roof. Plus, two other EPO cruiser escorts, one in front and one following, kept pace. Rooftop light bars with their red and blue lights blazing cleared the road by leaning on the occasional siren for drivers too blind to see the lights. They sped south down US-41. After a few turns, twenty-two miles, and thirty-one minutes later, they made their way onto Old Beartown Road, between the towns of Richmond and Lenox.

Sam drove as fast as safety allowed toward an old logging road "header" where logs were brought down to be loaded onto transport trucks. Glenn kept looking over his shoulder, growing increasingly nervous about Lumpy waking up. Elapsed time since his injection: ninety-five minutes. Then,

Lumpy groaned and started to roll. The van rocked in response. Sam could feel it in the wheel. They were still a few miles from their Plan A. Time for Plan B. They pulled over at the edge of the state forest instead of toward its middle. There were houses nearby, but this bear would feel right at home out here. Besides, they had run out of time.

The two EPOs jumped out of the big van, ran back to open the doors, and the bear reacted to the commotion, squirming in surprise. Sam said, "Oh shit, he's coming around." Glenn nodded and pulled on Lumpy's two dinner-plate-sized front paws. Sam wrapped his arm around the bear's neck to help get him onto the ground before he took off their heads. His arms reached only halfway around that soft barrel-neck. They dragged him out and the big fella dropped to the ground in a heap with a grunt. Sam pulled the damp rag from over the bear's eyes. He had secured it in place with a few loose wraps of duct tape. Glenn reached to check Lumpy's respiration when a mighty grunt issued from the bear's open jaws. Sam said, "Lookout, Glenn, his eyes are moving."

Sam was knelt close to one of those huge front paws when the bear took a slow swing at his face. Missed by an inch. Thankfully, Lumpy was still feeling the Ketamine/Rompum cocktail, or he'd have erased a good portion of Sam's face. The bear was on his back. Tried to stand up, but only succeeded in rolling over. Glenn glared wild-eyed at Sam and shouted. "Let's get the hell outa here." Sam slammed the van's rear doors shut. Lumpy jerked in response, and they both hustled back to jump into the still-open front doors. Both escort cars stood well off observing this little operation. Their job was done. They headed back to their respective stables.

Glenn and Sam both huffed from exertion and a little shock. They looked at each other and laughed. Sam said, "God, I love this job, at least at times like these. It is *so interesting*." They laughed again. In the rearview mirror, they watched the bear becoming animated. First, a stumble before he found his legs, and then he lumbered off the road and into the thick woods. Sam muttered, "God's speed, old fella."

Glenn took a deep breath. "Coffee? There's a great shop that also serves terrific cream cheese Danish in Berrington."

"I'm buying." Sam spun the van's rear tires on the gravel that shouldered Old Beartown Road.

*Another half-assed job well done.*

# 14

A week later, Liam Sullivan said, "Conor, we don't need no stinkin' job. We'll just live off the land." That was his way of saying they'd hunt prey that carried cash and cards, not to mention scoring some more high-end camping gear.

The head jack had fired them for missing too much work. "Boys, I need a crew I can depend on. We got schedules to keep. Dunno what you're doin', but you ain't doin' this no more. Here's your last paycheck."

Liam hissed, "Whatever." He snatched both checks. "Anyways, we're hunters, not jacks. We're outa here. C'mon, Conor." He wheeled away from his now-ex-boss and motioned to his partner. They slumped away, both kicking Mel's shiny truck fender on the way to their own with the soles of their heavy boots. "We don't need his shit."

---

They enjoyed the hunt. And now, it would be their profession—full time. Plus, they relished getting away with anything and everything. Part of scratching their itch. "What say we ditch the truck and hit the trail where them hikers are, Conor? Stay off the roads. Safer, too. We can always steal another one if we need to, with a full tank. If them rich weenies can hike the AT without a vehicle, so can we, right?"

Though Conor looked doubtful, he got into the spirit of the moment. "Sure, Liam, why not?" But he *liked* that rusty old truck.

# 15

July 2, 1988
   Somewhere on the Appalachian Trail
   Berkshire Mountains
   Northwestern Massachusetts

———

In the best shape of her life at forty-seven, Dr. Mary Bishop had begun what she called her *spirit quest* a month earlier. In another two months, she'd return to their dream home on Lake Tahoe. Mary and her husband Grant, also a psychiatrist and ten years her senior, sold their successful private practice and were debt-free for the first time in twenty years. They planned to work out their differences after this time-out. She wasn't sure, but suspected Grant was having an affair. He was gone *so much*. Or was she over-thinking what each of their respective passions had done to their relationship?

Friends mocked her for such a detailed plan to hike the longest trail in the world—alone. But that was Mary. Despite a lingering doubt, she smiled as she pictured her handsome husband pursuing his own dream at that moment. People paid to hear him speak. He was a foremost expert on aberrant psychology. Grant's twenty-five-city tour would consume most of the summer. And that was fine with her, wasn't it? Part of his publicist's plan to raise awareness of his new book, "The Psychopathy of Angry Adolescents."

They both loved their time apart, and soon, their time together again. She hoped... and feared. Starting in January, they looked forward to enjoying a beautiful rented house overlooking the Pacific Ocean from Point Loma in San Diego, one of their favorite homes away from Tahoe. Grant had found the perfect place. She'd complained they did not need a five-bedroom, three-and-a-half bath house. But the view was so perfect. He had sent her no less than seventy-two photos. Once more, she agreed to Grant's wishes. Just once, she wished....

. . .

Mary had started her "through-hike" of the Appalachian National Scenic Trail at its northern end on Mount Katahdin in Maine the first day of June. They told her that was a tough part of the AT. That's what the locals and experienced hikers alike called it. She'd done exhaustive research. Better to start hard than to end hard. Some said the AT was not only the longest trail at almost two-thousand-two-hundred miles, but also the most dangerous. The AT followed the ridge line of the Appalachian Mountains, ending at Springer Mountain in Northern Georgia. Everyone had advised she not hike the AT alone.

Other than her Grant, Mary needed no one. At five-foot-seven, she weighed in at a grizzled one-thirty-eight, proud to be a competitive kickboxer. She could take care of herself. Armed with a canister of bear spray, two knives—one for camp chores, another razor-sharp for protection—and a ton of attitude, she felt invincible. Out here, anyway.

Mary began her aggressive five-day hike over the ninety-mile western Massachusetts portion of the AT—the most rugged stretch. That part of the trail cut through the gorgeous Berkshire Mountains. The weather so far had been glorious, perfect for achieving the eighteen mile-per-day goal she'd set for herself. And now, she feared for her life—an unfamiliar and nerve-wracking sensation.

Her eyes darted as she scoured the dense brush around her for the source of her terror. Surrounded by shadows in the old-growth forest, giant ferns brushed both her legs from either side of the narrow trail. Claws raking on bark and an unnerving, deep-throated growl preceded her flinging her forty-pound backpack to the ground. The mesh pocket on its side held her large canister of bear spray at the ready. She pulled it out, tugged on the ring of the safety pin with her left thumb. It came free. The clawing and growling grew closer. Musky smells assaulted her. She froze in the dim light filtering through the forest's canopy. Then....

"Scat! Get out a here!" A gravelly voice hollered, unseen, but close.

Mary wasn't sure what startled her more. The possibility of crossing paths with one of the black bears known to live in this forested section of the AT? Or was it encountering a total stranger this far from civilization? City streets didn't frighten her.

Out of the brush appeared a man—short, dirty, and muscular, but his smile appeared sincere. Those eyes did not. In an instant, she estimated his height, weight, and physical condition.

*Yep, I can take this guy if need be. I think.*

Mary lowered the spray canister to her right hip, but kept her index finger poised on the activation lever as she returned the guy's smile. She said, "Hey, thanks, Mr.—"

A flash of light from a crushing blow to the back of her head interrupted what would be her last words spoken aloud, but not her final thought. *How could I be so **stupid?***

# 16

J uly 6, 1988

Sam's boss, Lieutenant Paul O'Neill, asked the Massachusetts EPO Inland Enforcement Bureau dispatcher to patch him through to Travis's radio in the field. "Sam, we got a missing through-hiker up on the AT. Missed a check-in with her husband two days ago."

He *was* enjoying a peaceful ride up near the summit of October Mountain, keeping an eye out for post-holiday poachers. He had a plan to familiarize himself with a new trail cleared a few months ago under some recently erected power lines and towers.

The shades of verdant green exploded around him on this brilliant summer day. Even so, a few leaves had dropped and swirled on the blacktop ahead of him. "Seriously, boss? Hikers go missing or are overdue all the time, especially on the AT."

"Well, this gal's husband says she's as regular as the Naval Observatory's Atomic Clock—his words. Plus, she's some kind of heavyweight west coast doc. So's her antsy husband."

"Say, what? Why me?"

"Husband says she's reliable, almost obsessive, and she's *never late*. Says she's really late. Coordinate with the Berkshire County State Trooper's barracks. They're the ones who asked for you."

"Okay, yeah, that'd be Lieutenant Rick Smith. Helped him out a while back. Thinks I'm a tracker. On it."

---

Regional EPO Office
Glenville, Massachusetts

Sam wondered how his desk could be so messy when he spent so little time here. Worked from home most of the time. Picked up the phone and dialed. "Lieutenant Smith, it's Sam Travis. Got a ghost on the AT, I hear."

"Sam! Hey, thanks for callin'. Gettin' some major heat here. Doctor Mary Bishop, a through-hiker, disappeared in our neck a the woods at least a couple a days, now. She was last reported buying provisions three days ago—Sunday, over the holiday weekend—and then, nothin'. Hell, I'm not sure where to even start on somethin' like this. Me 'n my troopers run damn fine speed traps, and got an outstanding record of workin' with our county animal control at findin' lost pets, but this?"

"Okay, LT. Tell me what you've done so far, and we'll go from there. Fair enough?"

"The husband, Dr. Grant Bishop, flew into Pitts-field last night on a private charter from Albu-querque. He's in the middle of some sort of speaking tour. The guy's a mess, Sam. Up on Greylock, well, you know."

"LT, from the beginning, okay?"

"Sure thing. Well, I had a couple of troopers hit grocery stores, outdoor supply stores, and trail outfitters in Williamstown. Branched out four miles from the local AT access point. We felt that would be about the maximum hikers would go out of their way. Showed each outfitter a picture of Dr. Bishop. One in Williamstown identified her. Picked up supplies totaling $153.22. Nothing out of the ordinary. The clerk said she was nice, relaxed, a gracious lady. Said she was headed south to hit Mount Greylock and looked forward to the hike. Used the pay phone outside according to the clerk. We believe she called her husband. The timeline matches. That's it. Nothing since."

The MSP lieutenant sounded exhausted and worried. "That's a good start, LT. Nice work. I'll drive up from Tyringham in the morning. Gotta tuck my kid in tonight, delegate some other business, and muster a few supplies in the morning. Get some sleep tonight, and we'll hit it tomorrow. Meet you at your office, first light?"

---

Sam hung up and pulled a few topographical maps from his files. Williamstown nestled in Berkshire County's Hoosic River Valley near the Vermont border. Highlands surrounded this village of a few thousand souls. At the northern end of the Massachusetts section of the trail, Mount Greylock loomed to the south on the topo map. With its summit at almost thirty-five-hundred feet, Greylock was the highest elevation in the state, and covered a lot of rugged square miles. But every search starts at one point—where the missing party was last seen.

# 17

S am beat feet up to Cheshire to work with Lt. Rick Smith of the MSP to investigate the disappearance of Doctor Mary Bishop. As standard procedure, they did a background check on her with a federal database called NCIS—the National Crime Information Center. Clean. Also checked on her husband—just as clean—but learned he also held a five-million-dollar insurance policy on his wife. Sam and LT considered that a possible motive. But there were no commercial flights from any US city on the husband's speaking tour to anywhere near the site where she disappeared in Western Massachusetts. They looked at private flights, too, but found nothing. The man had an alibi. Gun for hire? They kept digging.

Their initial investigation suggested a debt-free couple. But Sam discovered through his banker friend that Grant Bishop took out a mortgage on a five-million-dollar house on the shores of Lake Tahoe. Turned out to be a false trail. They eliminated the hubby as a suspect, for now. Still no corpse, anyway.

Sam started his search, with help from Lt. Smith and his troopers. He spent two entire days hiking the trail Mary Bishop had traversed. They did not find her body, but discovered a canister of bear spray with her prints on it. Sam refused to believe this was evidence of a bear attack. The sprayer hadn't been used, although someone had pulled the safety ring. They found that nearby. Curious. Its location was consistent with where she was last seen, her scheduled checkpoint, and no sightings further downrange on the trail. Her pack and any other trace of her was missing, too.

An intensified search of that area revealed no further evidence of foul play. Others believed she had wandered off the trail, got lost, and curled up to die. Sam did not. He dove into Doctor Mary Bishop's life, her habits, interests, and her extensive planning for this trip, per her husband. Not some naïve, ill-prepared woman, Mary was hard-core prepped and knew her way around hiking gear and campsites. By looking at a dozen more photographs provided by her husband, Mary kept herself in amazing shape, *and* competed in kick-boxing tournaments. Hardly a piece of fluff, this woman. She was a survivor. Unless....

Doubt clouded Sam's mind. Another week passed. His boss, Lieutenant O'Neill, suggested they treat this as a missing person case only. They found no evidence of foul play—none—and he put pressure on Sam to move on. "It's a state police job now, Sam."

"But boss, she's now one of mine."

# 18

While Sam searched for a missing hiker, Agent Kim Mason of the US Fish and Wildlife Service sat behind a modest desk in his small office in Boston's Korea Town. His feet crossed on top, staring over the tip of his left shoe at the prim and proper and oh-so-stiff assistant US Attorney Richard Lowry. They agreed to meet in Mason's office, not in AUSA Lowry's Boston office at the Department of Justice, District of Massachusetts, down at 1 Courthouse Way. No prying eyes up here. And Mason was one of the few agents at the Federal Wildlife Service who maintained a private office outside of the US Federal Wildlife Service's Northeast Region HQ in Hadley, Massachusetts, a hundred miles east near Springfield. Part of his cover. Even featured a small window. Now, he read the letters backward in small black letters the name of his cover business through the frosted glass door over the arrogant AUSA's left shoulder. It was backwards, of course:

*Lassiter Exports*

Lowry looked out of place. Like the president visiting a trailer park. He didn't even hide what he thought of this space, dominated by Mason's tiny desk and chair, one guest chair, and three filing cabinets. You'd have thought he suffered from inhaling the odor of something rotten. *Tough shit, Counselor. For what I pay you....*

The man always looked camera ready. Unless he was returning from a weekend in Atlantic City. Lately, word was he'd been haunting the MGM in nearby Springfield. Stood out there, too. Even then, the AUSA wore shirts so stiff they'd stand up by themselves. Count your fingers at shoulder level in the reflection of his thousand-dollar Oxfords. And he ensured the diamond links restraining his monogrammed French cuffs were visible from afar. Those rocks were as large as small walnuts. *What a pompous clothes horse. But his bad habits keep me out of jail.* Mason didn't look worried. Still, he asked, "So how bad is it, Counselor? Captain Jamison is no slouch."

Lowry's every move appeared to be orchestrated by some invisible screenplay. Thoughtful hand to chin. After a moment of sincere reflection, it descended to meet the other at his collar. His blue power tie with bold diagonal stripes in gold, each bordered by a burgundy pinstripe, showcased a perfect full-Windsor knot. He engaged both manicured thumbs and forefingers to micro-adjust it. Dropped his left hand onto the right knee of his crossed legs. The right now rose to emphasize his point. *Jeez! What, already? This guy!*

"Agent Mason, it was foolish of you to get caught. I pulled some strings in acquiring that writ to release you into my custody. Not to mention the challenges associated with the seizure of your two boxes of files. Even though we recovered them after I forced their release back to you, they likely examined them, or worse, made copies. I need to know of any other vulnerabilities we might be facing."

Mason appeared more confident than he felt, but no way he'd give this prick the satisfaction. "Not to worry about that, Counselor. They're coded. *And* written in Chinese Mandarin."

Lowry looked confused. "But... you're Korean."

"Yup. Even if they're able to translate it, we use a cipher that only an NSA analyst could break. And even then, they'd *still* not know what they were looking at."

"If Jamison presses, are there any other soft spots to cause us worry?"

"My superiors at USFWS trust me. I can do no wrong. In the last few years, I've busted enough low- to mid-level players that they give me free rein. Travis and Jamison killed my last crew, so no worries there. And neither my domestic distributor nor my Korean network have anything to gain and everything to lose by betraying me. So, we're good, right?" He slapped on a contrived smile to reinforce his high-energy optimism.

Lowry winced at the blunt description of so many crimes, but cleared his throat and muttered, "Excellent."

"So, how was Atlantic City? Or was it Springfield this time?"

"How—?"

"I'm a cop, remember, Counselor?"

"That is none of your affair."

Mason detected a crack in his demeanor with his quick answer a quarter-octave higher than usual, but the attorney recovered in the next instant. A hardly noticeable momentary lapse in his smooth exterior. Except that the fingers of his hands now danced on his right thigh. A superb lawyer, but Mason guessed this guy was a lousy gambler. Strange for someone who lied and argued for a living.

It was time for the man to beat a hasty retreat. He gathered his elegant overcoat from the back of the guest chair. Snatched up his top-loading brief case from the floor to his right. And he admonished Mason over his left shoulder as he reached for the door knob three short paces away. "Stay out of trouble."

*What am I? His delinquent son?* "I'm a federal agent, Lowry. Don't you forget that. You continue to earn your keep and we'll be fine." The man didn't like being reminded he was under Mason's thumb. Lowered his eyes and left without uttering another word. *I'll have to take measures with this suit at some point.*

# 19

Sam watched the Mary Bishop case stagnate for lack of evidence, and a body. He'd met with the Massachusetts State Police Lieutenant, Rick Smith, visited the woman's last known location, and they had searched with dogs, but found nothing. Not satisfying, just reality. Her husband offered a reward and plastered flyers in every town and AT shelter across Western Massachusetts. The guy was hurting. Impossible to imagine what he was going through. Even if she was dead, lack of closure eats away at survivors, especially a spouse. It ate away at Sam, too.

He slipped back into his normal routine. There

was an AT cabin on Upper Goose Pond and a couple of great ice-cold springs where hikers filled their canteens. No need to filter *that* water. He worked a boat patrol detail on Goose Pond during a scorching mid-July weekend heat wave. Lots of people and boat traffic this time of year, which was why the lake association there—that Sam helped form—hired EPOs like him for patrol details on the lake and surrounding roads. Parking was always a problem and it often got so jammed up that a fire truck couldn't get through on Lakeside Drive and Cooper Creek Road should the need arise. That was a problem, and that meant towing and writing a lot of citations at fifty bucks a pop, plus the cost of the tows.

At about 1:30 PM on an early July Saturday, Sam navigated through the narrow channel between Lower Goose to Upper Goose in his official center-console Boston Whaler. Not a lot of traffic there—too shallow for larger vessels. The majestic surroundings captivated his imagination every time. Sam cruised the Upper Goose to cool down. His dark green uniform, ninety degrees, and ninety-percent humidity conspired to incite heat exhaustion. A local TV meteorologist had predicted a scorching summer day on the morning news. For once, the weatherman nailed it.

Sam nosed the boat to shore, nudging its bow onto the tiny sand beach. No need for an anchor—no wind, secluded, and remote. He crawled out over the bow of the seventeen-footer, its ninety-horse-power Yamaha outboard raised to its stops. With a towel in hand, he headed for the cool spring up toward the edge of the woods forty feet away on this little peninsula. This was also a popular watering hole with AT hikers. Needed to douse his head and splash cold water on his neck. The spring maintained a forty-eight-degree water temperature year-round. After ten minutes, he returned refreshed to the boat, but it was... gone? The Whaler had drifted away from the shore. *Shit! Gotta swim for it.*

He stripped off his full duty belt, gun, boots, uniform shirt, shoes and socks, but kept his uniform pants on. No way was he leaving his pants behind. He swam to the boat in less than a minute. Even though it was only a lousy hundred feet, his pants filled with water and drew him down. Climbed into the boat via its stern ladder, lowered the motor, and returned to shore in about fifteen seconds to retrieve his gear.

About the time Sam got dressed and geared up again, a boat screamed through the narrow channel he had navigated thirty minutes earlier—a no-wake zone. So, he shoved his Boston Whaler off the tiny beach, hopped in over the low bow rail, lowered the motor again, lit her up, hit the lights and siren. Stopped the guy and his three wise-ass friends. Sam was already in a dark mood.

The kids continued swilling beer, like this was cheap entertainment. Officer Travis flipped a couple of fenders over his railing between their two boats and secured a short midship line between them to prevent them from drifting apart. Gave the young man behind the wheel a stern look and said, "Registration, please. You understand what you did, right?"

"Yep. Hey, Officer, it's hot, but why are you dripping wet?"

As Sam started to write the ticket, he muttered, "Need to know info, and you don't need to know."

They laughed, shook their heads and slapped each other fancy high-fives. Sam's jaw tightened. Wrote a ticket that would cost these smart-asses a couple-hundred bucks and said, "Get off the lake. Right now." They stopped laughing. He followed them to the boat ramp to ensure they complied with his "terminate voyage" directive.

Sam was drying out. He indulged in a chuckle of his own. Then he thought of every worst-case scenario for his missing hiker case—Mary Bishop. His mood darkened further.

---

Sitting in his home office six days later, Sam mulled over the sparse details, again, on Doctor Mary Bishop. A week of fruitless searching and nothing. Even the dogs found no scent. He stared at photos, a life insurance policy, and a transcription of interviews. Nothing inspired him. He grunted in frustration. Couldn't let it go, though.

Most EPOs had offices in their homes since they were spread so far apart. Kate worked at the newspaper and Brian was in school. Sam then resorted to trudging through his routine paperwork, beginning with his daily narratives which gave his supervisor, among other data, his Bronco's starting and ending mileage. Copied and filed all fuel receipts and expenses. He entered codes for the type of activity he conducted each day that included the number of contacts, warnings, citations, and arrests. Also, more mundane stuff ranged from caring and maintenance of state equipment, like firearm cleaning, cruiser maintenance, as well as time spent on court preparation, returning phone calls, and a host of other duties.

Sam hated paperwork, but he appreciate the need for it, *and* how it facilitated the job he loved (most of the time, except when it didn't love him back). Now, he couldn't shake the foreboding feeling that another girl was about to fall prey to a two-legged predator. And he was sitting here, inside, shuffling papers.

# 20

L iam Sullivan spent a lot of time living in the past, not that those were good memories. But even now, they continued to plague him. By the end of his senior year in high school during the late Spring of 1978, for example, he and Conor had become inseparable. The two of them talked at length about getting laid, by anyone, just to satisfy their lust. Then, just like that, they had graduated. Barely. They'd needed to go out into the big, bad world and earn a paycheck. No choice. Both of the boys were scared, although they'd never admit that out loud. Liam scored a job at Corey's Repair. Conor became a delivery driver. Both hated their jobs, but at least they did *not* follow in their fathers' footsteps at the mill. A minor victory.

Living at home became intolerable. The time came for Liam to square up with dear old dad. Liam approached his nineteenth birthday, now five-11 and two-hundred-twenty pounds of sculpted muscle. Looked as though his body couldn't get much bigger without bursting. Same with Conor. They even sported a few stretch marks. Liam knew he'd be leaving home. There was no love there. So arrived the night of his vengeance against the man who beat him and treated his mother and little brother like slaves. He waited until the fourth half-tumbler of Irish whiskey had done its work. Walked into the living room and delivered his pronouncement to dear old dad. "I'm leaving this shit-hole."

Liam's mother's eyes grew wide. She had known this day was coming. She grabbed Mac and said, "We're going for groceries."

Mac whined in oblivion to the developing drama, "Not now! This is my favorite show!" With a vice-like grip on Mac's arm, they disappeared from the house in record time.

"*Shit-hole?* Kid, you know how hard I worked to keep you fed and clothed all your life? *Shit-hole?* I oughta kick your ass."

"Try, old man." Michael Sullivan rose quicker

than Liam expected, and he took a short-handed right to his left cheek. It stung, but he took it and blocked the next two punches from his father. The booze slowed him down. Liam went to work. Liver shot, sternum, up to the face and back down to the body. It was over in two minutes. He left his father unconscious, blood oozing out of his left ear, mouth and nose. Packed up his things and left his mom a note:

> Dear Mom,
> Sorry bout your husband, but he deserved his own beating. I hope that Mac can protect you from him. I'm leaving for good and hope your life will get better.
> Love ya, Liam.

He left the house and moved into the apartment he and Conor rented with their first paychecks. They felt like kings. They both drove old pick-ups to get around, now had their own apartment, a little money, but still no women. They vowed that would change.

And now, ten years later, that night still haunted Liam Sullivan. He had abandoned his mom and little Mac at the vulnerable age of fifteen, left them in the clutches of that monster. If that drunk were still alive.... But Liam recognized his own truth. He was no killer. Oh, sure, he and Conor would have their fun with some skanks, but they left them alive. No, he and Conor weren't killers. Not really.

Two weeks ago Liam and Conor had worked their way south to the northern section of the Berkshire Mountains of Western Massachusetts, near the New York border. It was rugged, steep and exhausting. Worse, hanging close to the Appalachian Trail, their designated hunting grounds, their truck wasn't of much use.

Liam had said, "Conor, this piece-a-shit is too easy to spot, even though we stole it up in Maine."

"So, what'a we do, Liam. We gotta have wheels."

"Do we? I said it before. Why not provision along the way, like them snooty hikers do? When we get close to a town, we hoof it into one of the bigger stores. Besides, we're runnin' real low on money, and can't afford gas. We gotta find us another mark so we have some fun and take whatever's worth takin'. We snag their credit and debit cards. That'll buy us some goods."

"But don't cards leave some sorta trail, Liam?"

"That's good thinkin', Conor. But after a day or two, we ditch them cards, and we'll be long gone. Just gotta avoid cameras 'n such. What do ya think, man?"

"Cameras?" Now Conor got nervous. But then grinned big just as quickly. He had an idea of his own. "What say we use disguises to fool them cameras? ATM's got cameras, but we withdraw cash and beat feet, right, Liam?"

"Pardner, you ain't as dumb as you look."

Conor's grin transformed into a look of disappointment. He was never gonna be smart enough for Liam. Near Pittsfield, they hitchhiked to a brand new store nearby. Picked up a dozen candy bars, two six-packs of cold Bud Lite, a small styrofoam cooler, some maps, two cans of lighter fluid, and a fresh roll of duct tape. They'd abandoned the truck a couple of miles from North Adams. Wiped it down as best they were able, like they learned from their cell mate Lakeith in Albion. He also taught them that no matter how carefully they wiped something down, the cops'd still find some stuff, but he told them that fetched them get-away time.

They had headed south fast, away from Maine, where they knew their last victim might turn up. But the cops didn't know where they'd strike next. Hell, even *they* didn't know. The Vermont section was barren of hikers, so they had pushed on to a place called Mount Greylock where they partied with a nice-looking lady. Though she was older than they liked, they had some real fun, *and* scored some nice camping gear along with a chunk of cash. No plastic, though, which was weird. Or they just didn't find it before they ditched her pack.

After that, the boys decided to hole up near October Mountain State Forest—somewhere farther into Massachusetts, they figured. That's what the signs said, anyway. And according to the map they bought, that forest was a huge chunk of real estate. Plus, it had a campground only a couple of miles away, and that meant hikers. Probably families, too, but they wanted no part of *that*.

Now, a mile or two downrange from the campground, they came across a small clearing, and an even smaller pond—a sweet spot to set up. Close enough to the AT to hunt hikers, but far enough off the trail to remain undetected. Steered clear of a small swampy area to their north. After unrolling the sleeping bags and setting up their tent they had retrieved from their truck before abandoning it, they settled down to grab some rest after their long hike from the truck. Then, the hunt would begin.

# 21

Meanwhile, back in his glass-walled office in Wedgewood, Jeff Brahney rapped his fingers on his desk in sequence. He took refuge in his comfortable and familiar surroundings. Looked out at his small-town community bank's floor at the few patrons waiting in line at two teller windows. He thought about hiring another teller for the third window, but as long as the lines were shorter than four customers each, he couldn't justify the expense. With the soaring interest rates, business *had* been good, but lately... not so much. His assistant manager sat at her desk chatting with a customer. Applying for a loan? People were no longer borrowing like a few years ago. Inflation had taken a serious bite, and the general economy was down. This was all familiar territory. He knew the rules.

Now, though, he was about to venture into unknown territory. He'd gone to college with Marvin Clearwater, one of his few Native American friends, who had gone on to great things. Marvin was a supervisory agent of some sort at FBI headquarters in Washington, DC, for the money laundering and forfeiture unit in their investigations division. An assistant answered the phone. "FBI, MLF Unit, AD Marvin Clearwater's office."

Jeff's stomach belly-flopped. *Assistant Director?* For the tenth time in as many minutes, he asked himself what the hell was he getting into.

"Um, hello. This is Jeffrey Brahney in Wedgewood, Massachusetts. I'm an old friend of Mr. Clearwater."

"Please state your business, Mr. Brahney."

*Oh, shit! What **is** my business?*

"Well, I wanted to reach out to Marvin... Assistant Director Clearwater, that is. You know, catch up. We were classmates at Harvard."

Jeff thought he heard the woman smile over the phone.

"I see. Well, why don't you give me your number, and I'll ask the AD to return your call. How's that, Mr. Brahney?"

"Oh, well, yes, of course. Wonderful. Thank you."

After he spelled his name and gave the lady his number, he thanked her again and hung up. Then, and only then, did he stop sweating bullets.

The phone rang mere moments after he had composed himself. "Jeff, is that you? Good gawd, man, it's great to hear your voice!"

"Marv? Hey! Thanks for getting back to me. I wasn't sure—"

"Oh, yes, Denise is stone-cold dead serious about her job. You may imagine I am often deluged with calls. She's a marvelous gatekeeper, as they say. So, to what do I owe this distinct pleasure? No one ever calls just to *catch up*. But that's okay. I *am* a public servant *and* an old friend."

Now embarrassed, Jeff gathered his courage and said, "Marv, you've done well for yourself. Impressive. I'm only the owner of a small-town bank. Perhaps—"

"C'mon, now, Jeff. Let's have it. There's something rattling around in that large accountant's brain. You were forever the smart one."

Jeff smiled. He'd helped Marv when most everyone else at Harvard only saw an injun from the grassy plains of North Dakota, someone there on a politically motivated scholarship. But Jeff sensed something in Marv. His brilliant mind and incredible work ethic left no doubt that his friend's destiny pointed him toward greatness.

"Okay, here it is. A state cop friend of mine is on the trail of a DOJ employee. Convinced he's corrupt —an AUSA out of Boston, our old stomping grounds. Takes money from an international smuggler for get-out-of-jail cards. But my friend doesn't know who to trust, even within his own organization. He thinks there's a money trail that could convict this bastard—excuse the language. And my friend is also nervous about his own boss, though there may be nothing there. But we're punching far above our pay grades on this matter out here in Smallville. We're not sure where to turn. Ideas, old friend?" The silence over the line caused Jeff's stomach to flip-flop again. Then he added, "Marv, if this isn't an appropriate ask, I'd understand."

"No, no, Jeff. I'm processing what you've shared with me. I'm in the investigations division. I investigate. We conduct formal and informal inquiries, interview witnesses, examine brokerage records, review trading data, and use other methods geared toward investment inquiries. It's just that we don't normally investigate one of our own, even from within other divisions in the Department of Justice. But if there's rot within, I'm *personally* invested in *that*. The DOJ has made opportunities this scrawny old Turtle Mountain Chippewa from Rolette County would never have dreamed possible. This is now my house. How about you give me the info you have, and let me see what I can dig up? Fair enough, my friend?"

"Marv, that's more than I expected. Let me ask you. Do you ever miss school?"

"Are you kidding? At school, I was only some affirmative-action scholarship redskin. I remember in Cambridge, you were one of the few people who treated me and my heritage with deference. I owe you for that."

For ten minutes, Jeff explained the concerns Sam Travis had brought to him about AUSA Richard Lowry. He focused on the attorney's suspected relationship with a corrupt federal agent of Korean descent named Kim Mason. As a sidebar, he also mentioned Sam's commissioner of the Massachusetts Environmental Police, Tom Verdi.

After Jeff Brahney, small-town banker, hung up from his conversation with FBI's Assistant Director in charge of Money Laundering and Forfeiture, he slugged down half a bottle of Pepto-Bismol. He was now *way* outside his comfort zone. Hell, he had plopped his butt squarely into the danger zone.

# 22

Marvin Clearwater wanted to help his old college friend and protector from back in the day. But investigating an Assistant US Attorney inside his own organization was *way* outboard of his mission. He kept regurgitating Jeff Brahney's words. *A state cop is on the trail of a DOJ employee. Convinced he is corrupt. An AUSA taking money, bribes, from some international smuggler for get-out-of-jail cards. No idea who to trust, even within his own organization.*

*This target will be no Wall Street dummy. Like every AUSA, this guy will be a high-powered attorney who perches in the middle of a well-connected network.* A tricky dribble if he took it on. *But how can I not?* Jeff was a friend, but more than that, shared his own ethical bullseye. And he found it impossible to ignore a potential source of corruption within his own Department of *Justice.*

*Shit. Now who do **I** trust? I can't take this beyond an informal inquiry, and we'll need to be careful about interviewing witnesses. So, no formal order of investigation, for sure. No subpoena, which would leave a blazing paper trail....*

"Denise, please ask Agent Dunwoody to come to my office."

"Yes, Assistant Director. May I tell him what you need?"

"An informal inquiry with which I need help. Thanks, Denise."

"Yes, sir."

Clearwater trusted Pete Dunwoody to be discreet. He'd engaged him for unofficial inquiries before.

---

Five minutes later, Agent Dunwoody knocked on his boss's door after nodding to the AD's lovely assistant. "Denise, you look ravishing today."

She smiled. "He's waiting for you, Agent."

*Not the warmest reception. At least she smiled.*

"You wanted to see me, Assistant Director?"

"Come in, Pete. Close the door."

*Uh-oh, he only closes the door when we're going "off book." One of these days, this is gonna cost me my job. But I owe the guy.*

"What's up, sir?"

"Pete, we suspect a DOJ employee of corruption. I need you to discover whether there is credence to this claim—with discretion, of course. If this isn't a credible tip, we can't afford to disparage this man's reputation."

"Not our usual fare, sir."

"I know, Pete, but—"

"No worries, sir. Off the books. Name?"

"AUSA Richard Lowry."

Agent Dunwoody whistled. "An AUSA? Okaaaay. Wow. Timeline?"

"Let's say one week. Report only to me. Will that be a problem for you, Pete?"

"No, sir. On it. Anything else?"

"One more thing. Same gig for Tom Verdi, Commissioner of the Massachusetts Environmental Police. And I appreciate your discretion, Agent Dunwoody."

"My middle name. Sir."

# 23

Josie Currant was a junior at Lenox High School. In about six weeks, summer vacation would end and she'd be a senior. She tingled at the prospect. A senior! Jo, as only her closest friends called her, was a few days from seventeen, but looked like she was twenty-one. A gorgeous girl, and shy about that. Made her even more appealing, some said.

Josie had a lot of friends and treated every one of them like a gift. She was an honor student, a cheerleader, well-liked by her classmates and teachers alike. She didn't have a steady boyfriend. Rather, she dated a few boys—athletes. Josie admired boys who took care of themselves, like her. She wasn't a fitness freak, but stayed active, which kept her lean and taut. Plus, she respected her body and ate or drank nothing to pollute it. Her long blond hair and deep blue eyes were the envy of other girls in school. She never wore make-up. Didn't need to. Her skin was flawless. Her mom, Maeve, was also lovely. Even her father was a tall, light-haired, handsome engineer for General Electric. They were blessed and knew it.

After an early dinner, Josie hiked a trail at the eastern edge of October Mountain State Forest near their home. She loved the woods for the silence—a welcome respite from traffic noise, TVs, and the phone. She'd enjoy the warm July sun for another two hours before it set; enough time to get in a relaxing hike that would also get her blood pumping.

---

Liam and Conor finished their dogs grilled on a tiny alcohol camp stove they had acquired from that older lady a couple of weeks earlier. Tasted damn good after a long day on the trail. Washed them down with a few beers. The campsite was a short distance away from the trail, but far enough to avoid being heard. Thick brush heavy with blackberries, short pines, lots of white birch and oak concealed their campsite's little clearing from prying eyes. Decided to check their surroundings. Might get lucky. They'd walked a third of a mile. Liam placed his right arm across Conor's chest to stop them dead in their tracks, his left index finger to his lips. "Shhh... hear that?"

Conor stopped, listened, and bobbed his head. Faint humming of a tune they didn't recognize grew louder. A girl's voice. They ducked into the bushes, and as a stunning young blonde came into view, the young men's spirits swelled. They grew giddy with anticipation at the sight of this lovely piece of flesh in shorts and a tight tank top. She hummed away as her long strides up the steep trail delivered her to within a few yards of their hide. Her ponytail bobbed from side to side. Her long perfect legs glistened with a light sheen of sweat, as did her shirt, *and* what was underneath, they imagined.

She carried no backpack, and they didn't see any pockets. No chance for anything of value, other than what her tight little body was going to do for them. With no plan whatsoever, Liam waited behind that blackberry thicket until she passed them less than three feet away. He came up behind and slung her into a sleeper hold, cutting off the blood and oxygen flow to her brain. *God, she's so smooth and warm... and strong.* She struggled at first, but then went limp in his enormous arms after fifteen seconds. He liked to count off how long it took for someone to go limp. *That's power!* he thought. Liam scooped her up like a child's doll, slung her over his shoulder, and walked up the trail to their camp with Conor following.

"What if she wakes up before we get there, Liam?"

"I'll put her back out. Be ready to grab her legs, as I'm guessin' she'll be a handful if she comes to. She's really buff. If push comes to shove, a quick roundhouse to the temple will put her out again."

They hiked up the mountain. Josie regained consciousness after five minutes with a groan and a whimper. Liam plopped her down on the ground, delivered a vicious blow to her left temple. Slung her over his right shoulder again like a sack of meat. Less than fifteen minutes after they'd departed the trail, they arrived back at their campsite. Liam ordered Conor to bind and gag the girl with their fresh roll of duct tape. Conor winced at the bruise and swelling now raised on the side of the girl's head from Liam slugging her. Had to hurt. *But not as much as what's coming....*

# 24

Shadows lengthened as the sun descended into the trees to their west. Conor collected dried limbs from the edges of their little clearing. Liam snapped them and stacked it all like a teepee. Squirted it with lighter fluid, and used his trusty Bic lighter to set the wood ablaze. Meanwhile, Conor unrolled his sleeping bag near the fire. Both sat down on the bag and started pounding down beers. After a few, Conor felt frisky. Stumbled over to the girl. They'd propped her up against a big old birch tree. He said, "Yer jus' too damn perfect, ain't ya? We knew girls like you in high school, just too fuckin' perfect for real men like us." He drizzled some beer over her head. Not too much, though. Limited supply.

"Hey, what the hell're you doin', Con? Knock it off! Don't want her smelling' like stale beer. Spoils it."

It was as if Conor didn't hear him. Liam got up, walked over to his partner, who was still flapping his jaw at the terrified girl. Still drizzling beer on her head, flattening her wavy blonde locks on top. It ran down over her eyes and the tape covering her mouth. Liam delivered a semi-serious kidney shot to Conor's backside. That got his attention.

"Ow! The fuck, Liam?"

"I don't want her messed up. Not yet, so knock it off."

"Okaaay! Wasn't thinking." Rubbed his bruised side.

"No, you don't think. That's the problem."

Liam chugged the rest of his Bud, crumpled and tossed his empty into some long grass, untied the girl from the tree, and ripped off her tank top. With an appraising eye, he growled, "Well, looky here, Con. Let's get rid of these, too." He cut off her shorts with his razor-sharp knife, and tore at her panties as if they were made of tissue. Not much left, but ripped the remaining shreds as well, which raised a few welts on the girl's waste and thighs. But he left her hiking boots and socks. *Somethin' about a naked girl in boots.* He didn't like fingers and toes much, but bare skin... and *hair*? Now, *that* was something else. "Hold her down, Con." He leered like an owl about to descend on a field mouse for dinner—talons forward for the attack.

---

Josie regained consciousness. She didn't grasp what was happening, but knew she was in terrible trouble. Her eyes darted side-to-side, down at her own nudity, and up at these dirty monsters leering at her, keeping her clamped to the damp ground. Panic set in. She could not catch her breath, especially with something holding her mouth shut. Blood pounded in her temples and clotted in her nostrils. She wondered why she suffered from the worst headache she'd ever experienced. *Can't move. What's going on? Oh, God!* She screamed, then pleaded, but it all sounded the same. "Mmm, mmm!" But she stopped as she needed to focus on getting air into her lungs.

---

Liam ignored her, having ignored it all before. He thought, *No, no, please, please! Blah-de-blah. Always the same shit.* Conor grabbed her legs, Liam got hold of her still-bound hands. They half-lifted, half-dragged her onto the open sleeping bag by the fire. Conor popped another beer and sat cross-legged to watch. He saw the girl's eyes widen into saucers as she watched Liam now towering over her at full attention with his jeans clumped around his ankles. *They're never too good for me when I'm standing over 'em, are they?* Josie shook her head feverishly from side to side.

Conor watched this entire ballet of violence, smiling, swigging down the rest of his Bud, burping loudly now and then. Up close, now, Liam peered at the girl's almost-perfect hair, except for that idiot Conor's drizzled brew. He grabbed her hair. Ripped out the rubber band thing that held it back in a ponytail. Pressed a handful of her long hair against his face, and drew in a deep breath. *Hair is <u>always</u> special. This one's smells like strawberries. Gotta have me some.* He snatched his treasured hunting knife and whacked off a chunk of hair from the top of her head, wiped off the blood and beer, sniffed it again, and stuffed it into the special pocket in his nearby backpack. With the rest. He hardly heard the girl's whimpering sobs now.

They took turns. They were rough, callous, unrelenting. The girl almost immediately lost consciousness. Figured she was pretending. Didn't matter. Hours passed and the sun popped up. They had finally run out of beer and enthusiasm. Stood her up, but she was in and out. Carried her back over to the tree where they'd stashed her before the previous night's festivities began. Liam drew his knife from its sheath on his right hip to split her taped hands apart. "Gimme that rope," Liam commanded. He tied a length of their rope around the now-tattered and stained lengths of duct tape still stuck to her left hand, and slung it up over a hefty bow of that old birch, about eight feet up and off to her left. He tied it off to itself. Did the same with her right hand on the other side with a length of that same rope he'd hacked off. Spread her legs and tied 'em off that way to heavy brush on either side of that tree. Lots of scratches. Conor liked to scratch during the heat of passion.

---

Barely conscious, the girl looked dazed. *No wonder,* thought Conor. *We done give this one a pretty good workout.* Seeing she was coming around—again—on an impulse, Liam punched her in the stomach. No idea why. Seemed the right thing to do. "Perfect little bitch ain't so perfect no more, are ya?" Conor took his turn, too. Liam *screamed* at her so hard he left the ground once or twice with stiff arms and spread fingers. His spittle sprayed the girl's face inches from his own bitter mouth. "Slut! Pig!" He said to Conor, "We shoulda got more beer. I'm thirsty."

Inspired by Liam's bold actions, now from eight feet away, Conor bent over and grabbed a fistful of soft, almost gooey moss. Threw it at the girl. Struck her mid-chest and almost stuck, but then slid down her naked torso before dropping to the ground at her feet. She appeared to be unconscious again. All spread-eagled like that, it was as if she couldn't hold up her head anymore. Her whole body looked limp, like she was hanging from the ropes around her wrists. It *was* a lot colder this far from the fire.

"Nice pitch, Con. Lemme try that." It was like another frenzy came over them. They took turns chucking muck at her, each throw harder and more rapid-fire than the last. After several minutes, the fire in them subsided. Conor shuffled over to see if she still lived. He bent his ear next to her nostrils. Still breathing, but barely, now battered and near unconscious.

· · ·

Liam and Conor were drunk and sated. They fell onto their open sleeping bags. Woke up to a bright but foggy mid-morning two hours later. Both took in their campsite and the girl. She was a mess and out cold. Hungover and feeling shitty, they broke camp. Liam's head pounded. Said, "Check and see if she's still breathing, Con." Conor lost his balance, trying to stand up. After three tries, he stumbled up to the once-beautiful young girl. She looked like a different person. Blood, beer, muck and body fluids had dried over most of her. Matted her hair and crusted over most of her flesh. Conor took a closer look at the unconscious girl and heard no breath. Felt a pang of guilt. "Yeah, she's gone awright. Shit. Cover her up or somethin'?"

"Naw, let's get the fuck out of here. Leave her. We'll be long gone before anyone finds her." It took almost an hour to load their backpacks. They walked back toward the AT in a funk.

"Where to now, Liam?"

"Spotted a likely place on the map we picked up. Called Upper Goose Pond. Good water, close to the AT. We'll hole up there 'n chill a bit. Unless we get lucky again."

They shared an uneasy laugh and kept walking.

Didn't even look back.

# 25

Josie Currant awakened in the afternoon sometime. Her whole body convulsed in painful spasms. She realized she hadn't had anything to drink since yesterday. Struggled to see as her left eye was swollen shut, and blood crusted over her right eye from what felt like a deep scratch or cut above her eyebrow, or maybe from the top of her head. Burned like hot coals up there. Her subconscious mind told her she'd die if she didn't do *something*. Darkness would come soon.

So, weak as she was, she started slowly working on the ropes that bound her wrists. So tight, but she was slimy-slippery from what those awful men threw at her. In what seemed like hours, she loosened up her right arm enough to squirm out of the rope tied over the severed but slippery tape still sticking to her right wrist. Her arm fell limp to her side. After resting for a while, followed by more persistent effort, she freed her left arm the same way. Rested some more. Ripped the tape fragments from her mouth and wrists. Rubbed her wrists before she massaged both arms to regain some circulation. They hurt so bad and had turned a dark purple, but her eyes found no tears.

Exhausted and dehydrated, and grateful that her fingers worked at all, Josie spent ten more minutes freeing her feet. Her arms and legs and the rest of her body were in excruciating pain that preceded a creeping numbness. The cool July night air and her immobility for so many hours caused painful stiffness, and then cramps, like she'd never experienced before. Still, no tears came—wondered if she'd ever cry again. She was just... angry. And scared. Didn't know if those monsters were still in the area, or whether they were coming back.

Josie stood up, but fell right back down again. Tried again. This time, she kept her now-bare feet under her. No boots or clothes to be found anywhere and she had no energy to search for them. The sun set. Josie sensed which way was downhill—to safety. Took one hellish step after another. Not sure what it was, but something kept tearing at her bare flesh, something beside the cold air. Numb, she pushed onward, sometimes falling, sometimes heaving in what might have otherwise been called crying. Still no tears, though, only dry, jittery sobs. So cold. Her lower jaw chattered furiously. Uncontrollably.

After what seemed like hours of this stumbling torment, she spotted a faint light. A passing car? She shuffled along more quickly now. Kept falling and getting up. Always getting up. At last, she recognized East New Lenox Road. Followed the road. Josie knew it eventually intersected the Housatonic River. If only she made it that far, she could get a drink of water, at least. Spotted a dim light in the near distance off the right side of the road. It was a house she didn't recognize. Cold, naked, and more numb than not, she had little time before slipping into unconsciousness, and soon thereafter, death. A voice inside told her that.

Josie crawled on all fours up three porch steps and knocked. Nothing. She was too weak to knock more loudly. Saw a metal dog dish by the door. Slapped at that with a clatter on the planked porch floor and collapsed into a dead faint. Her last thought: *I wonder where the dog is....*

The overhead porch light came to life. The cabin door creaked open a crack. Charlie Granger, a seventy-five-year-old widower, peered out and almost fainted in shock at the mud-covered naked girl that had collapsed face down on his front porch. Charlie's combat training kicked in even though it had been almost forty years since Korea. Unable to lift her, he grabbed her arms and dragged her inside. As he did so, he huffed at the effort. "Sweet Jesus, you poor little thing. What some bastard gone and done to you?" Avoiding her most private parts, he wrestled her up onto his couch in that small living room. Fetched a glass of water from his kitchen tap. Fed her a few sips, but she didn't respond. He then dialed 911. *Shit, shoulda done this firs'.* "Help! Emergency! Come quick. Charlie Granger here, 75 East New Lenox Road. Got a poor girl here who dyin'. Real bad exposure. Deep bruised 'n bloody all over, but not losing much blood no more—at least on her outsides. She unconscious, but wif a decent pulse." Slammed the phone down, and fetched a light blanket. *Good Lord, who does such evil as dis?*

A Lenox Police cruiser arrived in less than five minutes. Two minutes after that, an ambulance arrived. The EMTs took the girl's vitals, started an IV to rehydrate her, covered her, and prepared for her transport with further triage. Two officers took a fidgety Mr. Granger outside, sat him on his porch swing. With a practiced professional calm, they acquired as much information as possible from the old man, thanked him for rendering aid, and for calling in. "Jus' find de sumbitch who done dis and kill 'em dead!" Charlie's veneer of calm cracked as he *screamed* this at the pair officers. They understood.

"Don't worry. We'll find the bastard, sir." Officer Flores seethed this pronouncement back at the old man. His hard eyes left no doubt he, too, was profoundly affected by what he'd seen this night.

# 26

That same night, Captain Larry Jamison reflected. Divorce did not agree with the EPO Academy Commandant. He missed Maggie, but she no longer missed him. The last few years had been rough. So they called it quits after twenty years. She took the house, and that was fine. He was never there, anyway. He got the six-year-old Dodge Diplomat and cheap rent payments on a one-room studio above the local hardware store on Main Street in Framingham. She asked for zero alimony. No kids, no child support. Heck of a deal. He was glad they parted friends. They were both ready to move on. Well, sort of. She was, anyway.

So, here he was. Forty-three and divorced, but

still married to his damn job. Self-esteem had never been an issue on the job. But sitting at O'Henry's in Framingham on a Sunday night, looking around like a solitary member of the lonely hearts club during Happy Hour? *Shit, what the hell am I doing?* And that's the precise moment his old high school flame walked in. Lindsey Magnus was with her husband, or date, or whatever. At least Magnus was her maiden name back in the day. *Damn, she looks good!* While her escort checked their coats, he caught her eye at the dining room entrance as she spotted him staring from the bar. *Shit!* He smiled and nodded. Noticed her eyes got wide, just for a second, before she smiled and nodded back.

He turned back to his beer, almost empty. Ordered another. Five minutes later, he felt a soft hand rested on his left shoulder. Turned on his stool's swivel, and there she was. "I thought I recognized an old friend," she said.

*Old friend? After what we went through together in high school?* "Linds, you haven't changed. It is *so* nice to see you."

"Hello, Larry. Talk about a blast from the past. I heard about you and Maggie. Small town."

"Yeah, it's difficult being married to a cop."

"Don't I know it. Bob was on the job in Boston

for six years. Killed in the line of duty nine months ago."

"Oh, Linds, I am so sorry."

"Long time ago. Truth be told, Lar', I didn't mind the job. Bob said he had a wife and a mistress. I told him as long as I'm the wife, I'll deal with his mistress—the job." Smiling with a wistful expression, she looked like she had overstepped, started backing away. "Well, I better get back." She nodded over her shoulder toward a table not visible from the bar. "This guy's not bad as far as first dates go, but he's no cop." She said it like nothing compared to a man with a badge.

"Thanks for stopping over, Linds. It really is awfully nice to see you."

"Bye, Lar'." And she turned to walk out of his life as abruptly as she had sauntered in.

*What the hell am I doing? Or **not** doing?* "Wait, Linds? Call you sometime?"

She turned back to look over her shoulder, but kept walking. Said, "Some cop you are," and pointed to the bar, but didn't stop.

*Is it my imagination, or does she now have more spring in her step than five minutes ago when she walked into the restaurant with that stiff?* He turned back to his beer, and there on an O'Henry's napkin was a hand-scrawled note:

## Linds
### 413-555-1969

*She must have scribbled that on this napkin before she even came over here. Son-of-a-bitch!* That got old sullen Larry grinning big. *Alright, then!*

# 27

Six days after calling his friend at the FBI, Wedgewood bank president Jeff Brahney heard from Assistant Director Marvin Clearwater. "Jeff, got some news. But you need to be careful who you share this with, *or* that you got it from me. Agreed?"

"Yes, of course, Marvin. What did you learn?"

"I've taken this as far as I'm able without raising red flags within the department, and that is a line I cannot cross. Tell your friend that one Richard Lowry has a serious gambling problem. And even though he's a married man, he is also a philanderer. My guy observed him three days this past week at the MGM casino and hotel in Springfield, meeting with some pretty seedy-looking characters and more than one woman. Not a straight arrow, and appears to be living far beyond his means.

"My operative even caught the exchange of a fat white envelope. But within the constraints of an *informal* inquiry, we have no visibility to bank transactions. I'm sure you understand. I *am* sending you some surveillance photos, including the negatives—overnight. It's all I have for you. Hope this helps, old friend. Oh, and the other gentleman, Commissioner Verdi? Appears to be a straight-shooter: family man, faithful husband, the guy has some political ambition, but my investigator saw no evidence of any indiscretions or malfeasance. As far as a quick look uncovered, anyway."

"Thanks, Marvin. This must have been risky for you. I appreciate your help."

"Pay me back by ensuring your cop friend gets this Lowry weasel. Corruption must not stand, *especially in this house*."

"I'll keep you informed, Marv. Thanks again."

"Don't worry, old pal. I'll know."

*Click.*

# 28

L ate morning the next day, Jeff Brahney wasn't in the mood for small talk. He sat behind his desk in his windowed office at the bank, like the day before, and the day before that, so he got straight to the point after dialing. "Sam, I have some information for you. Let's meet." Jeff had asked Sam's dispatcher to patch him through to the EPO's cruiser. He heard radio and car noise in the background.

"Sure. I'm tangled up in a missing persons case, an active ongoing investigation, but I'm back in town for the day to regroup." Sam wasn't willing to give up on the Mary Bishop case, despite his boss's edict to let MSP handle it. "How about Beverly's? I haven't eaten lunch yet. I'm buying. Fifteen minutes?"

"Deal." *Click.*

Beverly's Diner was only three blocks west on Main from Jeff's bank, and was *the* place in Wedgewood to get good food, strong coffee, and lots of street gossip. After swinging his bulk through the glass door, Brahney dodged and weaved around two busy waitresses burdened with loaded trays who scurried to booths in their respective sections, like every day, from open to close. One experienced waitress always balanced her tray overhead. He loved the nostalgic feel of this place that swept over him every time he walked through the door. Spotted Travis hunched in what he knew was the cop's favorite window booth with the mini-juke on the wall. Sam loved his rock 'n roll, even turned down low.

Like every hour of every day, the whole place reeked of coffee, corned beef hash, and fried eggs—in a classic diner sort of way. Almost covered up the stale smoke stench from old Jonas and Zeke puffing away at the counter. That was the smoking section, closer to the greasy ventilation fan on the side wall. Zeke was Beverly's son, God rest her soul. He had inherited the place. Said he'd never ban smoking. *Never say never, Zeke.* This was a rare sighting of Zeke outside of his kitchen. He'd hired some local teenager to do the heavy lifting in the kitchen for him. Small town.

Brahney slid into the booth across from Travis and got right to the point. "Hi. Listen, I want to get this out. My FBI friend down in DC found that your DOJ attorney is a serious gambler and womanizer. Hangs out at the MGM over in Springfield whenever he gets the chance. Lots of money changes hands. A *lot* more than a government lawyer makes. Like fat envelopes of hundreds, according to my friend's investigator."

Sam looked surprised. "No kidding. Any names?"

"No, but he sent photos." Jeff slid an eight-by-ten manila envelope across the table. "That's it, Sam. My friend crawled way out to the end of a limb here. Isn't even his bailiwick. He looks into stocks and bonds, certainly *not* high-level lawyers in his own backyard. Oh, and Verdi looks clean as far as their financial search went. My friend says to be discreet as hell about where you got this stuff. Do *not* put my friend in a world of hurt within the DOJ. You get that, right, Sam?"

"No worries, Jeff. This is great. I'll look at the photos later. What if I have follow-up questions?"

"Nope. You're on your own here on out. Okay?"

"Sure. Hey, I wanna thank you and your friend, man."

"Then honor your commitment. Buy me lunch. I have my eye on that chicken-fried steak special slathered in white gravy."

Travis grinned. "Deal."

---

Thirty minutes later, Sam shook hands with Jeff, who turned right out on the sidewalk in front of Beverly's. Sam took a left and jumped into his Bronco three cars away. Still parked on a diagonal facing the curb, like all the cars on that side of the street, Sam sat in his driver's seat with the windows open and the engine off. He squeezed together the two metal prongs that secured the manila envelope's flap and pulled it open. Inside were a half-dozen eight-by-ten glossy photos— black and white —of Richard Lowry, the guy who kept Kim Mason out of jail and from being prosecuted for myriad crimes including murder: accessory before *and* after the fact.

Mason, the corrupt mid-level US Fish and Wildlife undercover operative, almost got Sam and his boss, Larry Jamison, killed last Fall. That smooth-talking scumbag was at the heart of a conspiracy to traffic millions worth of illegal animal parts on behalf of a South Korean distribution network. Both Travis and Jamison *knew* Mason and Lowry were dirty together, but they had had no proof at the time. And Lowry pounced on that lack of physical evidence like a vulture on carrion in the middle of the damn road. Mason had been out on the street ever since.

Sam looked at the first photo of Lowry shaking hands with a slick-looking dude that Sam didn't recognize. He'd find out who this slicker was, though. Looked mobbish. Lowry was in the second photo, too, playing five-card stud. Nothing incriminating, other than he nursed a tall stack of... yellow chips? Those were worth a thousand a piece. But when Sam saw the third photo, he grinned like someone had handed him his case on a silver platter. Looked like a narrow hallway leading to a fancy men's room. It was a photo of Kim Mason handing a *fat* envelope to Lowry himself. The next photo was even better. A close-up of Lowry's hand featured his fancy Yale class ring and one monogrammed French cuff. In the close-up photo of the money and the ring Sam clearly saw it spelled:

*R.F.L.*

Richard. Fucking. Lowry. The photo showed him pulling a crisp bundle of bank-bound hundreds from an expandable envelope to examine the goods. Whoever took these photos was one hell of a surveillance expert.

"Gotcha, you slimy shit!" A lady walked by on the sidewalk in front of Beverly's, just outside Sam's open driver's window and turned at his exclamation. He winced, caught her eye, puckered his cheeks, and nodded his apology.

The next photo showed Mason poking his finger into Lowry's chest and swatting the hand holding the envelope like he was lecturing a foolish child. Lowry appeared disheveled, possibly inebriated.

A couple more photos featured the normally prim and proper AUSA sloppy drunk with a top-shelf working girl hanging on him. The first caught him at a blackjack table shoving a tall stack of yellow chips toward the dealer. In the last photo, he entered an MGM hotel room with the same thousand-a-night hooker. Looked like a million bucks. She kissed him, embraced him around his neck, and explored territory south of the equator... in a damn hotel hallway. He quickly opened the door and they disappeared. *Party time, Counselor? For a slick federal mouthpiece, why not learn a thing or two about discretion, you crooked piece of shit!*

Sam felt the bile bubbling back to the surface. This slimy dirtbag protected the criminal who ordered his partner murdered, who held the leashes on a crew of poachers that tried to kill him and Larry. *I <u>will</u> see you rot in hell, Counselor.*

# 29

Two days later, Captain Larry Jamison was hot to meet with Lt. Paul O'Neill and his favorite smart-ass EPO, Sam Travis. They were to discuss what some in the press were now calling the *Trail Predators Case*. Now, with a surviving victim, there was new hope. Larry pushed his old Dodge Diplomat a little harder than it deserved or tolerated. He needed to get away from his office at the EPO Academy in Framingham, anyway. He'd taken the commandant's job to satisfy his wife. Maggie was now living her own life, but he had committed to this job for at least two years. So be it. He still stayed involved in cases he cared about

—with EPO Commissioner Verdi's blessing. Best of both worlds.

The trip to their regional office in Glenville from the EPO Academy in Framingham would take about ninety minutes from Route 91 south to the Mass Pike west. Larry set the cruise at seventy-five for smooth sailing. Grabbed the exit south toward Westfield State College and a right on Court Street.

That's when it happened.

---

Larry awakened in the hospital. Some drunk had T-boned his 1982 Dodge, they said. No airbag. If he'd owned a Chrysler a few years newer.... *Might just buy one, now that some idiot totaled the old Dip*. He was lucky, they said. Further bruised a couple of already-injured ribs from a gunshot wound last Fall (there had been a few complications), displayed a helluva shiner—two, in fact—and cracked his Roman nose. Left arm hurt like hell, and both wrists got bruised from getting tangled in the wheel. But he was alive and almost still kicking.

"Captain Jamison, we're gonna keep you for a few days. Other than what we call a full-body trauma from the side impact that caved in your driver's door, your injuries aren't serious, as of today. You *must* take it easy, though, and give your body time to heal. Or the consequences—"

"Got it, Doc. So, when will you send me home?"

"We'll see. Right now, I'm thinking day after tomorrow at the earliest. Now lay back and get some rest.

---

Larry got a call the following day. He took it from his hospital bed. He was officially assigned IOD status by the commissioner—Injured On Duty—based on his condition. Not optional. The commissioner wished him well and a speedy recovery. Larry called Sam at his home in Tyringham. "I'm out of action for awhile, Sam. Sorry."

"Take care of yourself, Lar'. Anyway, O'Neill got a call from the commissioner's office. I'm to partner with a feeb on this Josie Currant case in a few days. I just know in my gut it's connected to the Bishop disappearance. And I'm betting this feeb is prettier than you. Commissioner Verdi and the Boston FBI SAC say we need a profiler on the case. With the potential for a multi-state jurisdiction, no choice."

"Now, play nice, Sam. Focus on getting your man. You got this, and you have a plan."

"Yeah, I just hope this *plan* isn't a shit sandwich minus the bread. Meantime, I got a few things to take care of."

---

Somehow, Larry's old high school flame, Lindsey Magnus, found out he was in the hospital. He'd been meaning to call her after she gave him her number that night they ran into each other at O'Henry's Steak House in Framingham a couple of weeks earlier. He'd mentioned her to Sam and suspected his pain-in-the-ass EPO had found her and called her.

No sooner had Larry hung up the phone when he heard his hospital room's door squeak open. "Linds? What are you doing here?" He became self-conscious about his appearance. She smiled without saying a word, approached his inclined bed, and brushed her fingers through his unruly hair as if he were a little boy who forgot to use his comb. She bent over and kissed his forehead. Stood up, reached for his right hand with both of hers, and squeezed. He just laid there, dumbfounded. Finally, she spoke.

"Oh, Larry, you look like that time in Driver's Ed when I was behind the wheel and hit that fake fire hydrant on the driving range. I got so shook up, I ran into Mr. Cheever's personal car at the edge of the course. You were in the back seat and hit your head on the front seat. Mr. Cheevers, in the passenger's seat, turned purple, waving his clipboard around. He was so angry at me for wrecking both the school's only Driver's Ed car *and* his own car. Remember that old piece of crap? He thanked me later as his insurance bought him a much nicer personal vehicle."

After recovering from Lindsey's surprise appearance, he grinned at the memory they shared. He also loved the way his stomach lurched seeing her again. "Hey, Linds, sorry for not calling after seeing you at O'Henry's. I intended to. Got tangled up at work, and then... this." Motioned with his left hand toward his wrapped chest. "How'd you know I was here?"

"Somebody named Sam—"

"Yeah, Sam Travis, one of my officers. A nosy bastard—pardon my French."

"Well, please don't be too hard on him. I'm glad he did. Gives us a chance to catch up." Larry decided he wanted to do more than catch up. Decided she was more than an old friend. Maybe a lot more. Time to take a chance. "Linds, would you like to have dinner with me once I escape this prison?" He motioned around the room with his left hand. She still held his right with both of hers. They were warm. But as he finished asking her, he felt her hands jerk. *Oh, shit.*

But then she squeezed harder and said, "I'd love that. I thought you'd never ask, ya big dope."

# 30

S am took it upon himself to surveil AUSA
Richard Lowry after receiving the incriminating information on Lowry from his
banker friend the day before. Wasn't sure why he
wanted eyes on, other than this asshole was part of
the conspiracy that got his partner killed the
previous Fall. And he just had to get his own eyes on
a piece of this crook's dirt. Ordinarily, a team is
used to surveil a high-priority suspect. But since
this was *way* off the books, Sam would do this
alone.

Per Jeff Brahney's FBI source, Lowry favored
mid-week days, Tuesday through Thursday, to drive
the ninety miles from Boston to Springfield, staying

one or two nights, but not every week. So, Tuesday, it would be.

---

Security at most casinos set high standards with cameras everywhere, and good-quality ex-cops both behind those cameras and on the casino floor who knew their way around. Sam would take no chances standing out. He'd use one of his more effective and simple disguises. But he didn't want Lowry to recognize him, either. Neither did he want to catch casino security's attention.

So, he dug the longish-hair blonde wig out of his undercover box of tricks. Wore a baseball cap, jeans, sneakers, didn't shave for a couple of days, and wore a plain sweatshirt zippered up halfway over a buttoned shirt to conceal a body camera. Nothing fancy—a look consistent with a lot of folks who hang out at casinos, other than the high flyers in the VIP rooms. Despite what Brahney's FBI source told him about Lowry's expensive habits, sounded like he favored the crowds of the main casino floor most of the time. Perfect.

Over the weekend before his planned stakeout, Sam had hung out at home with Kate and Brian. Both had raised their eyebrows as he emerged from the bathroom with blonde hair. Kate hoisted one eyebrow, smirked, and sputtered, "New look, cowboy?"

"Yeah, I'll be gone for a couple of days on the job, but should be back Thursday night at the latest."

"That gonna be dangerous, Dad?" A trio of Mason's poaching crew, enabled by Lowry, kidnapped Brian last Fall. The thirteen-year-old was more a part of his dad's profession now because of that, but also feared more for his dad's safety than before.

"Naw, Bri, just staking out some fancy pants who's doing some illegal stuff. Piece a cake. That's also why I'm not shaving for a few days." As they sat at the round kitchen table eating corned beef and cabbage for dinner, one of Kate's few specialties, Sam sat next to Brian, with Kate on his other side. He leaned toward his son and whispered loud enough for Kate to hear, "The beard and hair thing are part of my disguise. Cool, huh?" He circled the top of his head with an index finger, like he was tracing an invisible halo.

"Wow! Undercover, huh? Cool. But listen, Dad," Brian sculpted a serious frown into his face, "Kate and I want to be sure you're gonna be *real careful*. Okay?"

Sam smiled at being lectured by this serious

young man. His heart swelled. He felt awful that he'd let his work come home to haunt them all. He was so proud of both Brian and Kate for having come through that experience without too many emotional scars. At least that's what he thought. "You got it, Bri."

He smiled over at Kate. She was brimming with pride over how mature Brian sounded. But frustrated that despite what he said, she suspected he would put himself in harm's way. Again. Without a second thought. She added her two bits. "That goes double over here, Officer Travis." She reached to her right across Brian to grab and squeeze his hand. Held it a few beats longer than either expected.

Casino time. Tuesday afternoon, Travis hopped in Kate's car, an American Motors Pacer, instead of his official Bronco. He'd thrown the Wedgewood Courier magnetic signs from the doors into the back —face down. The Bronc broadcast law enforcement. Kate's Pacer mumbled blue-collar civilian. He aimed the squat little two-door toward Springfield, eighty miles down out of the mountains. Didn't go this long without shaving unless he had a damn good reason. Now he was reminded why. Scratched his stubbled neck. Itched like a damn rash or something. But nailing Lowry made it worth the discomfort. He already had enough to make the man mighty uncomfortable, but when you went up against a slick lawyer like him, a little extra insurance never hurt.

So, he meant to hang out at the MGM casino for a couple of days at the most. He couldn't get that lousy scene at the Wedgewood Superior Courthouse last Fall out of his head. They had nailed US Fish and Wildlife Service agent Kim Mason dead to rights. The man ran a multi-million-dollar illegal wildlife harvesting and exporting ring while working at Fish and Wildlife. Mason recruited and employed poachers who had killed his own EPO partner, Sergeant Frank Murdock, almost got him and Larry Jamison killed, and had kidnapped Brian. *Plus,* they beat up Kate—in his own kitchen. Yet this asshole Lowry somehow got a writ that said Mason was only doing his job as a Federal Wildlife Service undercover agent to inform the DOJ of illicit activities. *What a load of BS.*

And sure enough, there he was. Spotted AUSA Richard Lowry—a *married* DOJ representative—

living large at the MGM, hanging with hookers. *I wonder if his wife knows.* The man placed one bet after another *no* government employee could *ever* afford, especially as Sam watched this guy lose time and time again. Yup, Sam had seen enough, just in his first night surveilling this slime bucket.

As Sam looked around the casino, he suspected Lowry was already being tracked by the feds. Because what had started as an informal investigation, his banker friend's FBI source told him, Lowry was now under the DOJ's official microscope. For all he knew, DOJ investigators were watching the crooked lawyer right this moment, like him. Of course, Sam didn't spot them if they were. Nor did he take any pictures. Already had those. And as soon as the US Post Office delivered his second copy of those pics, so would Lowry. If called to do so, Sam was now a potential *eye* witness. Time to call it a night and let the feds do their thing. They had the case's lead, anyway, not state-level guys like him.

True to his word, Travis had not revealed to anyone where he got the incriminating photos of AUSA Lowry accepting a bribe. But Sam had made no promises what he'd do with them. He had made two copies of each image at his local photography shop. Kept the negatives at his home office, mailed one copy to the Office of Internal Affairs at the Department of Justice, and the other to Richard F. Lowry's office, to his personal attention: eyes only. Obviously, Sam had worn gloves while handling this evidence. The FBI forensics crew would be all over it searching for trace. He also knew he could not be tied to any of this. These photos would get Lowry's attention when they arrived in a day or three. Sam called this *shaking the cage.* Also, he did not know if Jeff's FBI friend mailed those photos to the right people himself, too, but suspected he had. Didn't matter. He'd done his part. That helped, if only a little. He'd rather have his hands around this bastard's windpipe.

---

In the following days and weeks, the feds would leave Jamison and Travis out of everything. That was typical, anyway. They confirmed through an independent source (Jeff's FBI friend) the DOJ *did* initiate a formal investigation, and on the strength of those anonymous photos, obtained a federal warrant, and gained access to Lowry's bank accounts. The DOJ took internal corruption seriously.

Four days after Sam's little off-the-books surveillance sortie, their investigators called in the FBI SWAT Team to surround Lowry's house. A single car in the driveway. The Chevy SUV registered in his wife's name was nowhere to be seen, and the garage was empty as SWAT observed through a side window. Thermal imagery confirmed Lowry was alone in the house.

The Special Agent in Charge and on-scene commander used a loudspeaker encouraging Lowry to surrender. The SAC preferred a peaceful resolution, but from surveilling the AUSA's house over the previous twenty-four hours, they observed Lowry was in a volatile emotional state. Nobody is as deaf as someone who doesn't want to listen. And that's when they heard the gunshot. The SWAT team breached—front and back. Found Lowry dead at his desk from a self-inflicted GSW.

Five minutes earlier, Lowry ran through his options. Surrender, face the press, arraignment, indictment, a public jury trial, maybe grand jury, certainly divorce, humiliation, sentencing, and life in prison, likely with slags he'd put away himself, even in a white-collar camp. Or opt for the coward's way out. So, after swilling down a quart of Pig's

Nose Scotch (surprised himself that he favored this cheap brand for day-to-day use), he shoved the .45 against his right temple and pulled the trigger. Spilled the remainder of his final drink all over his note, rendering illegible.

The feds controlled the fallout.

# 31

Travis learned of Lowry's suicide the next day. He drove over to Boston. It was time to end his and Larry's unfinished business from the previous Fall. He had learned from Jeff Brahney's FBI source and his investigator that Federal Wildlife Service Agent Kim Mason kept an office in Boston's Korea Town, in the Allston area south of the turnpike and Beacon Street between Harvard and Park Vale Avenues. Nice address. For Korea Town. Travis had found him in his element— his undercover identity. And since the feds kept Lowry's demise out of the media, no way the rogue federal Fish and Wildlife agent had yet learned of

Lowry's suicide. Travis watched Mason's office the entire afternoon.

Travis was no stranger to tailing someone. It remained an art form seldom appreciated, even in police work. They taught it in many academies and advanced police procedural courses, yet few excelled at it. Sam did, but he needed someone to tail. So, he surveilled Mason's export office for six hours.

Persistence, patience, and luck conspired against Mason, in favor of Travis. Simple things like weather, traffic, and the number of people in an area contributed to a successful tail once surveillance paid off. Standard operating procedure when undercover? Travis wore a reversible coat he'd change periodically. And he rotated between different hats while tailing Mason after the scumbag would leave his office, a third-story walkup. Sam was more at home in the woods than on big-city streets. But a successful tailing operation favored Boston's heavy foot traffic—Mason's element—as Sam transitioned from his surveillance hide to following this crooked agent.

Minutes before sunset, the sky darkened with the cloud deck lowering. Rain would help. Then, thirty minutes later, Mason emerged from his building on Portland. Ever cautious, he scanned the street, trying to spot anything that didn't quite fit.

Travis saw him watch several people hustle to their cars to hop onto the Southeast Expressway for home before the rain caused the inevitable gridlock. Traffic was already snarled, bumper to bumper. Slow going as usual. Such was Boston at rush hour. It seemed Mason saw nothing to trigger caution or alarm.

Sam kept a hundred feet back and to his left, looking into a men's store window across the street from his target. He wore no baseball or other hat just then, only his trusty high-collared reversible jacket —white on one side, dark blue on the other. Travis had discovered Mason loved Italian food even though he was of Asian heritage. Would he hit Regina's on the North End? Yup, appeared so. Maybe he was on his way to meet somebody over a plate of Regina's legendary Osso Bucco.

Sam was now close enough to hear Mason's fancy shoes deliver an audible *clack* with each step. Hunching over a bit more to further disguise his height, Travis wore jeans and sneakers. Decided to slap on a Red Sox cap and a pair of tinted eyeglasses to change up his look. After five minutes, Sam dropped back, just in case, but kept pace.

He stayed a suitable distance behind. If Mason turned off to one of the many alleyways, he would still be in range to catch up, but far enough back to avoid detection. If Mason stopped and turned around, Travis would continue walking or he'd get made. If Sam stopped and pretended to look for something, an experienced operator like Mason was sure to spot such a tell. The jerk stopped, turned, and scanned the people around him, one by one, but didn't react to anything unusual. Hunching over a bit to disguise his height, Travis switched his jacket from white to dark blue as the skies turned darker and threatened to pour. Took off his Red Sox hat and switched to a brown LL Bean. Mason stopped and turned again. This time, he got fidgety, but he was looking off to someone across the street from Sam. Not one to take chances, Mason picked up a little speed and checked again. Sam was glad the asshole thought someone else was tailing him. Took the heat off of him.

But soon, Travis became leery. This stop-and-go action flashed a sign, and not a good one. Something spooked the guy. Maybe nothing more than a twitchy instinct. The little hairs on the back of Sam's neck prickled. The worsening weather had started as a sprinkle, then increased to a steady downpour. If he kept Mason's pace much longer, the guy was sure to spot him. If he fell back again in this weather, he'd lose him. He stayed close.

Mason had the funds and the job that allowed him to leave Boston for however long he wanted. His superiors had grown accustomed to his tactics and considered it normal because he busted a lot of low-level criminals. He thought he was safe, but doubt now reared its ugly head. His pulse quickened. Suspected he'd picked up a tail. *Shit!*

He'd been on his way to meet a supplier in the North End. He expected a handsome profit from connecting this red neck with his own South Korean exporter. Couldn't take any chances. He veered off his normal path into an unfamiliar area, into a narrow cobblestoned alley off Haymarket Street. It surprised Mason that he'd never traversed this alley before, less than a mile from his office. Then, the sky opened up in earnest.

Now in unfamiliar territory, doubt crept into the agent's consciousness. In his haste to shake or ID his tail who demonstrated skills too good to be a dull mugger, he'd quick-turned into this narrow, dimly lit alley. Turned out to be a dead-end. *Good.* The sun had sunk and everything was now in deep shadow, further obscured by the rain. The street lamps kept the deepest shadows at bay on Haymarket, but not in these twisted eighteenth-century alleys.

His experience told him if someone was following you, by vehicle or on foot, make two lefts and a right. If they're still with you, get to a dead end. And here he was. One of three things could happen. You've been made and you confront the issue—escape or fight. Or if no one shows up, you're good. At least you'll know, unless you have a tail that waits you out. Worst case: you get eyes on your tail. Best case: no tail.

Mason charged at a brisk pace deeper into this alley full of delivery boxes and trash from adjacent restaurants. The cobblestone alley had been littered with debris, garbage cans, dumpsters, a derelict sink, a bicycle with a bent frame, and other dumped items. Lots of great hides if an ambush became necessary. Who tracked him? A simple mugger after all? No problem there. He'd beat this mongrel down. But anyone else? He had to know. He hadn't survived this long as an undercover operative and as an entrepreneur trafficking in contraband by being naïve about such things. Only way out? Through his tail. He turned to make his stand, still not knowing who this shadowy figure was. *What? That pain-in-the-ass EPO, Travis? How—?*

# 32

Travis peeked around the corner of a trashy alleyway Mason had ducked into. There he stood, thirty feet away, staring right at him, like he was expected. *Shit!* He bobbed his head back out of sight. The cobblestone street, like most of North End's streets, was littered with debris, garbage cans, dumpsters, derelict sinks, bicycles, and assorted garbage. Before entering that alley, however, he speed-dialed his boss's boss, Captain Larry Jamison. "Larry, I'm in a dead-end alley off Haymarket in the North End near the Public Market. Got Mason cornered. Send local PD backup, like fuckin' yesterday. Out." Slapped the flip phone shut, stuffed it into his jeans pocket, and entered the alley. Game on.

As he sauntered into the mouth of the alley with

deliberation, he looked up. The old brick buildings were close together, about four stories high on both sides. "Hello, Mason. Been awhile. Nice night." Rain dumped a steady stream off the bill of his dirty Boston Bruins cap. It was really coming down now. The alley's pitted cobblestone surface looked glossy.

"Cut the crap, Travis. Why the hell are you tailing me? Haven't you been humiliated enough with your amateur moves?" But Mason didn't like the sneer that appeared on this country cop's face.

Raising his voice loud enough to penetrate the distance and the rain now drumming off garbage can lids, Sam said, "The only way out a here is through me. And *that's* not gonna happen. Say, *Kim,* by the way, you haven't heard the news? Didn't get the memo from the DOJ? Your pal, Lowry, just blew up his career and both your lives. Seems they found out he's as corrupt as they come. They busted him for all kinds of nasty shit. Charges include conspiracy, and oh, accepting bribes from some rogue federal agent. Not to mention an accessory after the fact for the murder of an environmental police officer—my partner. Did you even know Frank Murdock, Kim? Yeah, Lowry lived *way* beyond his means, especially some of his recreation in Atlantic City and Springfield. And did you hear that in his *suicide note,* he must have experienced some pangs of guilt, bared his black soul before pressing a forty-five to his right temple? Then, one simple trigger pull. Coward. But he *did* tell us in his note about a couple of boxes we seized the last time we hauled in your punk ass. We made copies, of course, and he failed to demand their return. Some attorney *he was*. Turns out he didn't like you, only your dirty money. Said something about your books being coded in *Mandarin*? Clever, but... hey, I'm rambling, aren't I? Any of this trivia ringing any bells, Agent Mason? Yeah, we got a pretty good analyst from the NSA working on your transaction log as we speak. Translation? Your goose is cooked and charred, you crooked son-of-a-bitch."

That last bit was pure fabrication, but Sam wanted to watch this Mook squirm. The terror now clear in his eyes, they darted from side to side and revealed the microsecond evaluations taking place in his head. Conclusion? Naked fear. *Good*.

"You're done, Mason. Conspiracy, accessory to Frank Murdock's homicide before and after the fact, plus a few more. You're going away for life without parole." He'd been stalling, waiting for backup.

Something snapped inside this corrupt agent's head. Like a bull snorting before a charge, Mason advanced on Sam in mid-sentence with a feral roar, picking up speed the closer he got. Several things came to Sam's mind in that instant. Per capita, more Asians engage in extensive martial arts training than Caucasians do. Wasn't sure if that was true, or part of some cultural stereotype. But he'd already witnessed such skills in a few of Mason's known associates during an encounter a month earlier in a baggage-handling room at the Bradley International Airport in Connecticut. And even *they* were more advanced than his own training. *Watch his hands. Are his fists balled up or are they open? Open is more likely to suggest martial arts training.*

Sam was proficient in hand-to-hand combat training from his time in the Marines, on-the-job training and experience more recently, and he grew up fighting on the streets. He was a brawler and counterpuncher. And he fought left-handed. That could be an advantage in the initial stages of a fight. Mason snarled, "You can't take me, you country fuck!" *Off center, almost sideways stance, open hands, not fists. Shit.*

Sam growled. "Stop talking, asshole. Let's dance." Sam commanded good hand speed and reaction time. Because he was a cautious brawler, he crowded Mason to minimize the power of his sure-to-be devastating leg kicks. If he practiced Muay

Thai, an ultra-violent martial art, the guy would target Sam's legs and shins. Just walking would bring tears to his eyes if he let that happen.

Mason led with a roundhouse right leg kick. He spun around and missed. Followed it with a couple of feints and attempted hand strikes. Sam jeered. "Not even close. C'mon, Mason. Bring it." Sam launched himself at Mason with an overhand right. He expected Mason would block it, but the asshole never saw Sam plant his feet to leverage his entire body weight. Delivered a solid power left hook to Mason's liver. The corrupt fed buckled. But then he recovered and countered with a left kick to Sam's right leg with lots of follow-through, connecting above the knee. The sweet spot. Pain shot up to Sam's back. They both returned to their stances.

Each had sustained a solid hit. Sam again became the aggressor, counter-punching and crowding. *Gotta keep this guy's legs out of the mix.* On the balls of his feet, Sam landed a right to Mason's sternum, and a perfectly launched left hook to his mouth. That set Mason back against the brick wall, hurt and surprised. He sneered at Sam through bloody teeth. With a now-angry series of blows, he rabbit-punched Sam's face and delivered a vicious chop to his neck. That stunned him. Mason leveraged that opportunity to sustain his attack. Tried a leg kick, but the close quarters, crowded between Sam, the wall, and knee-high in trash, stifled much of its energy. Sam caught that leg and held on. Lifted Mason into the air and tossed him to the street, where Mason's head slammed onto the age-polished cobblestone.

Most street fights end in less than five minutes. Bleeding and winded, both men sought their second wind. Mason's skills exceeded Sam's, but Sam could take a shot as well as deliver them. Once more, Mason targeted Sam's legs with quick and vicious kicks, followed by hand strikes and close-in elbow blows. Sam envisioned the huge welts already rising on his calves and thighs from those kicks. One solid connect with one of Mason's elbows, and it would all be over. But right now, the pain exploding from his legs made it difficult to stand, much less to move. He was losing. Sam dropped to one knee. Tried to regain his composure with his chest heaving from exhaustion and pain.

*Is this the way I go out? On my fucking knees in this filthy alley? At the hands of this shit-bag?* His mind flashed back to his unfaithful Mother and the beating his father gave her long-haired drug dealer. All the rest came boiling to the surface, too. The anger of countless fights in the high school gym and outside behind the bleachers. The loss of his mother, his father, and most recently, his partner, Frank Murdock. He remembered his grueling hand-to-hand combat training and the Marine drill instructor who pounded him into submission so often it was a blur. All the beatings he gave and took since then, and arrests he had later made that turned into brawls. The more he flashed on all of this in the seconds he foresaw his own death, the emotional brutality of it bombarded him. If he lost here, his son Brian would be fatherless. He knew how deeply the boy would regret being robbed of any chance to say goodbye to his father. Each precious second of thought intensified a fierce passion, an anger, like a rising storm. *This ass-hat will not defeat me. Gotta get up off my ass and fight! If I don't cheat, I don't want to win bad enough.*


Mason smiled through bloodied teeth, smelling the sweet scent of victory. Whipped out a switchblade. *I guess he wants to win.* Rushed Sam, still down on one knee. Meant to finish him with a lethal kick to the head. Or a jab downward with that knife into his chest. Or if he got close enough, a quick slice across his throat and carotid. Or a jab in the back if he was too close. Each of these options required one leg to be firmly planted, from which to launch his final attack. The rain pummeled them with a steady downpour, now making the cobblestone alley floor slick as grease. Mason advanced on Sam, who drew on some unexpected reserve and rose to his feet. Mason planted his left foot en route to his target, now less than four feet away. He jabbed with the blade. Failing to connect, he made two lightning-fast slashes, first to the right, then to the left. Missed with both big swings as Sam sucked his gut away from that deadly blade. But then Sam surprised Mason by kicking that blade from his hand on a follow-through. *I bet he never expected* that *from this hick cop!*

Mason now moved more cautiously, antici-pating more kicks. *He doesn't know I'm in this much pain. Show confidence!* Now Sam saw the events of the next few seconds unfold in slow motion in his mind's eye. Body slam this asshole into the wall behind him. He'd go down. Then he'd mount him and serve up the vicious bile bubbling up from within. He'd come down on this corrupt fucker like an F5 tornado. *No way I die here tonight! But someone will.*

Sam executed. Mason sidestepped, but Sam's wild momentum drove Mason first into the wall, then down to the cobblestone. The man's head struck the stone again, stunning him. Sam straddled him. Used Mason's ears as handles. Smashed the back of the criminal's skull into the cobblestone with every bit of his remaining strength. Once. Twice. The rain didn't care, diluting both men's blood in crooked rivulets.

Sam then pounded Mason's face with a ferocity born of a lifetime of anger, danger, and disappointment. Again and again. He felt his power increasing as the mental vision of those he loved and lost increased the strength of each blow. Sam landed a vicious right elbow to Mason's mouth. He rearranged or sent Mason's teeth flying. Mason tried to throw Sam off, but he was too dazed and weak. Mason grabbed one of Sam's hands to set up an arm bar. But Sam was still the stronger and more agile. He pulled free. Mason grew ever slower and less energetic from Sam's powerful blows. Accelerating the sequence of right, left, right.... He'd found some new reservoir of destructive energy.

When fighting the type of man like this who lives by deceit, lies, and violence, Sam knew he must be prepared to kill him. Because there was no other way to beat him. He intended to kill Mason, not arrest him. He realized that now. The fury inside him raged like a forest fire driven by hellish winds.

Mason lost consciousness. Still, Sam's punches rained down on this murderous monster as torrential rain dumped down onto this pair of warriors from a leaden sky that didn't care who survived. Blood meandered down the alley in small rivers, now guided by the cracks between the rough cobblestones. Sam noticed shouting behind him. Four arms stopped his continued deluge of violence. It took both men to drag him off of Mason's motionless and battered body.

---

The firm arms and gentle voice said, "It's over, EPO Travis. He's done. You need to stop." One of the two Boston Police officers didn't look surprised by this extreme violence. He'd been there himself. He felt less compelled to save this criminal's life than preventing a good cop from committing murder.

---

Bruised and battered, Sam felt the rage receding. He wheezed from exertion and from a sore throat. Realized he'd been bellowing in rage at Mason with all the force his now-near-shattered vocal cords could survive. Sam then gazed in distraction at the uniforms, as if coming out of a rancorous trance, but said nothing. He nodded as he wiped the blood and rainwater from his eyes with the back of a soaked jacket sleeve. Didn't know or care if it was his own or Mason's. He'd lost track of his favorite Bruins hat.

The officers released Sam's arms. Two EMTs tended to a battered, bloodied, and unconscious Mason. Two more pulled a gurney from the nearby ambulance that had arrived. "I'm Sergeant Williams, ninth precinct." Travis said, "Sarge, not sure if I will thank you for preventing me from doing the wrong thing or be pissed for not letting me finish."

Williams replied, "I understand. Believe me. We got a call from Captain Jamison from your outfit who gave us your approximate location. I assume that once they're done with this turd, you'll want to arrest him formally, mirandize him, and haul his ass off to jail. I don't think he'll be hearing anything like his rights for a while. From what Captain Jamison tells me, there's little chance of bail since he's a flight risk and a mountain of serious capital crimes faces him at arraignment. FYI, after the hospital, he'll be transported to Boston City Jail. He'll be in an isolation cell, suicide watch protocols, the works. Is there anything else I can help you with?"

"No, but thanks again for your, uh, intercession and assistance. He killed my partner and is an accessory to three other murders, conspiracy, and a shit-ton of other charges I'm too tired to mention."

"Can't say I blame you for a little retribution, but I'm glad we got here when we did, even if you aren't. I don't think he'd be breathing if we were another minute out. You okay, Travis?" Sam was too tired to answer. Shook his head, like he tried to undo his lust to kill Mason.

One of the Boston PD officers with gloved hands showed Sam and Sergeant Williams Mason's loaded stainless Smith and Wesson Model 60 in an ankle holster. Two speed loaders and cuffs had nestled in a small back pouch on a belt they stripped off their prisoner. When they emptied Mason's pockets, they found his Special Agent badge and photo ID, along with some weird-looking pills, in a small container.

Sam acknowledged Mason's personal effects with a tired nod and mumbled, "Stick it in an evidence bag, fill out the form and start a chain-of-custody on that shit."

"Yes, sir." The young officer waited for the nod from his sergeant and left. The rain had let up and a slight drizzle now fell on Sam's head. He raised his face to the rain with closed eyes and stood there, leaning against the alley wall. It was either that or collapse. *Why didn't Mason use his piece? Pride? Vanity? A superiority complex?* Sam wondered why he didn't use his own gun, either. Never even thought of it. This was way too personal for both men. It needed to end like two gladiators—primal and savage and up close.

Sam felt the rage subsiding. Asked for the DA's office number. One of the EMTs said that the man on the ground needed at least a dozen stitches, along with X-rays of his jaw, skull and arms. *Concussion, no doubt, and about a dozen trips to the prison dental reconstruction team.* The older BPD officer asked, "Wanna get checked out, Officer Travis?

"Nah, I'm banged up, but okay. But a ride to my cruiser if you've got the time?" The Sergeant said, "Listen to me. Let this EMT clean you up. You're a mess. You'll scare the civilians. Besides, I think she's cute and could probably use the practice. Then, I'll give you a lift to your cruiser. We're glad to help, and don't worry. We'll have a police detail outside this dirtbag's hospital room and we'll keep him cuffed to his bed until you arrange his transfer to Boston City Jail. I'll help you with that, too."

"He's dangerous, Sarge. Tell your men to be aware that this man won't hesitate to take your men out."

"Uh, I don't think this guy will be too much of a threat. You've likely kicked that very shit right out of him," he said as he grinned, "but we'll watch his ass."

The tech blotted, butterflied and bandaged Travis. Handed him a couple ice packs for the swelling on his hands and face. Sergeant Williams watched with concern. Said to the EMT, "Nice work, young lady. Officer Travis, I'm around the corner when you're ready."

Sam flexed his swollen leg with caution. Those damn leg kicks, crowded as they were, caused him excruciating discomfort. He refused to think of it as pain. He limped his way back through the rain-soaked alley. Called Captain Jamison on his flip-phone. "I got him, Larry. Boston PD stepped up big-time." As he said that, he shook the BPD sergeant's hand, wincing at the pressure on his bloody knuckles. A minute later, Williams' unmarked cruiser disappeared into the night. Sprayed water everywhere as he transported the busted-up EPO to his own car still parked in his stakeout location across from Mason's undercover office. Sam continued his conversation as they drove. "Larry, get a search warrant for his office and take everything. From what Lowry gave us via the phone tap, we know he encodes his records Chinese, so we're going to need a good linguist to decipher it."

"You okay, Sam?"

"Yeah, I'm okay. A little busted up, is all."

"Sam, what the hell were you doing out there by yourself? Lemme guess—this guy kicked your ass, but then you got lucky. Am I right?"

"Yeah, sorta."

"Goddammit, Sam, this lone wolf shit's gonna get you killed. What were you thinking?"

Didn't mean to raise his voice to his boss's boss, especially in front of this sarge from BPD as they drove, but he did. "Look, Larry, I wasn't planning on making an arrest. I was following the guy to spot his new poaching crew."

"Shit, Travis, we got plenty to bust his ass already. When is enough, enough?"

"*Alright*, Larry, I get it."

"*Do you?* Sometimes you're the most savvy EPO I got, and other times you act like a damn shiny-boot rookie."

Sam seethed. Not because he was mad at Larry, but because he knew he was right. "You done, boss?"

"No, I am not. Get this. When you're out in the woods, you're alone. By necessity. But when you're in the fuckin' city, you work with me, the locals, the staties, I don't care, but we work as a team, and we work smart. City's different, you *know* that. *Now* I'm done. Good collar, Sam. Remember what I said. Copy?"

Sam mumbled his response. "Yeah, copy, boss. Loud and clear. Sorry. Hey, Boston's finest is dropping me off at my car now. Gotta go, boss." *Click.*

With Lowry dead and sufficient incriminating evidence from the seized files, Mason was indicted, convicted and sent to a comfortable prison—Fort Devens Federal Prison Camp—for white-collar offenders. He'd last a month at most in a general-population prison. But it was still prison, gen-pop or not. And Mason's imprisonment delivered some vindication for the death of Sam's partner, for beating Kate, for kidnapping Brian, and for his minions almost killing him and Larry, too.

Done and done. Next case?

Sam stopped at a drug store while still in Boston's Korea town to buy a bottle of aspirin. His head was killing him, and figured it might help with the inflammation everywhere. He was wrong. Drove the three hours back to his cabin outside Tyringham in the dark, ten percent conscious of the Mass Pike rolling by, at most. When he got there after midnight, both Kate and Brian stood on the porch with the lights on. Sam was slow getting out of his

Bronco. Stumbled to the steps. Tried to hide his pain, but failed. Both Brian and Kate helped him up the stairs.

Before he said a word, Sam said, "You should see the other guy."

"Oh, Sam, we need to get you to a hospital. You're—"

"I'm okay, Kate. EMTs patched me up. Hey, Brian, grab me a beer?"

"Not till we get you to the couch, Dad. Jeez, you look awful. You... *won*?"

"Kid, I'd laugh, but it'd hurt too much. Yeah, I won. Bad guy's arrested and on his way to jail."

"Why didn't you use your gun, Dad?"

"Brian!" Kate scolded him, grinned at Sam with her own questioning eyes, but said nothing more. They seated him on the couch in front of the fire.

Sam winced and smiled. "Now, how 'bout that beer?"

# 33

S till recovering from the street fight with Mason two days earlier, Sam felt surprisingly good considering the punishment Mason had administered. He'd nailed the kingpin who orchestrated the death of his partner the previous Fall. Finally.

With Larry out of action for at least the next several days, and the now-obvious kidnapping nature of their *Trail Predators* investigation, Larry and Sam Travis's direct boss, Lieutenant Paul O'Neill told Sam he was to partner with some hotshot profiler from the Bureau named Special Agent Letty Mather. Word from on high. They met outside his Glenville office and leaned against his

Bronco's front brush guard. At least she was nice enough to drive over. And she was easy on the eyes. He'd reserve judgment. They spread the case file documents and photos across the Bronc's hood.

The petite Agent Mather appeared to be as tough as she was attractive, in a manly sort of way, but feminine at the same time. She responded to his appraising look. "I gotta be tough to survive in the original *good old boy's club,* Officer Travis. Try being a vegan on top of that. Might as well be from another planet trying to play nice with the natives." Occurred to him she wore little makeup to downplay her natural beauty, more like good looks. Suit with pants, crepe-soled loafers, the works.

"Vegan? What the hell is that?"

"I eat nothing that once had a face or a parent. And that includes their progeny. Decided to stop treating my stomach like a junkyard *or* a graveyard."

"Say *what,* now?"

"No meat, fish, foul or dairy. It's a whole thing. But I love greens, beans, berries, mushrooms, onions, nuts and seeds. Weird, right? But I feel great. Less than half a percent of Americans are vegans. *I come in peace."* She hoisted a mock stern face and aimed a *Live Long & Prosper* hand signal reminiscent of the character Spock from the TV series, *Star Trek.*

Then she smiled and shrugged. "Yeah, I'm a 'trekkie,' too. So, sue me."

Sam rolled his eyes, shook his head, but concluded his little opera of body language with a quick mini-shoulder-shrug, a snort, and a grin. "Hey, you're not bad for a feeb, Special Agent Mather, even though you *are* a certifiable weirdo." She play-punched his right shoulder and got right down to business.

They had gotten word from Massachusetts EPO Commissioner Verdi himself, who received a request from the FBI Special Agent in Charge in Boston. Sam's reputation as a tracker and body recovery expert preceded him. Plus, he knew the mountainous area in question better than most anyone. The pressure to solve this now-suspected-serial was mounting—fast. All resources to bear, they said.

"Enough with the 'special agent' crap, Officer Travis. Call me Letty."

"Okay, Letty. I'm Sam. So you've examined the recent case file on this Josie Currant." Of course she had. "What do you see?"

"You mean besides an officer of the law standing in front of me who has suffered a loss, and is not sure what to do about his future?"

"What, now?" He swung his head from the files to stare at her - full frontal - thinking he'd heard her wrong.

"Sorry, occupational hazard. I read people. You lost a loved one, but now you're considering moving on. What's holding you back? Guilt?"

"How—?"

"Your pale band of skin on your left hand's ring finger. You wore a wedding ring there until recently. But now, you rub the back of that finger with the tip of your thumb. Force of habit, or you're anxious about no longer wearing that ring. Someone new in your life, maybe? Have you popped the question yet? Is she okay with your job? Looks like you just crawled out of a frontline foxhole. Job takes priority over your personal life, doesn't it?"

"Jeez! Alright, already. How about you profile our perp on this case? Have you read the file or not?"

"Yes, of course. Again, sorry. First, I think we're looking for two perps, not one." This surprised Sam. He didn't have to ask. His expression drew her explanation. "Look closely at these photos of the poor girl's arms and legs. They restrained her with sticky tape, maybe duct tape, right? Per the MSP report. But look at the pattern of abrasions from being bound for awhile—one to two days, based on her dehydration. I'm guessing she struggled at first, but not much. She was weak and scared, maybe unconscious based on the wallop she took to the side of her head. Someone slapped the wraps on her legs in a frenzy, *sloppy* wraps, and later obviously cut them off. But someone *neatly* wrapped her hands. See the clean edges on those abrasions? Likely two different psychopathies, here. One merciless and haphazard—he'd be the alpha. The other..." she sought the right words, "thoughtful, reticent, even sympathetic, but does *whatever* the alpha wants. Probably without even being asked."

Sam sort of saw the difference, but remained skeptical. "A reticent rapist?" She ignored his reaction *and* his tone. She still scoured the photos.

"And look at these bruise patterns. Yeah, she struggled at first, a little, even though she was bound. Some pretty deep bruising around her neck, and on the soft tissue around her shoulders. You don't restrain someone around the neck *and* around the shoulders with your hands at the same time, probably from holding her down during...." She didn't finish the sentence. Didn't need to. Couldn't. "The two repetitive but different bruise patterns could have been caused by the same person, although not likely. *More* likely, two different patterns created by two different perps. The file indicated she had indeed been brutally and repetitively abused...." Letty gazed off into some distant thought, maybe even a memory. Then she got back to business. "No, these are two different bruise patterns inflicted by two different people. Consistent with the two varied patterns of restraints. One unconstrained, the other restrained, but both actively involved. I'm sure any DNA evidence will confirm that, whenever that comes back from the lab."

"You see all that from abrasions and bruises?"

The FBI profiler continued without responding to Sam's half-quizzical, half-admiring grimace. "They didn't kill her, but came close and left her for dead. They've raped as a team before. Too well-organized for first-timers. Location, restraints, shaken beer sprayed up into the girl's vagina to flush—or at least obscure—trace evidence, per the lab... urban legend only, by the way, but part of a clear 'signature.' And they're young with wild libidos not easily sated. I'd speculate mid-twenties to mid-thirties. Assuming this isn't their first rodeo, they're likely convicted felons, probably for rape and aggravated assault. And they most certainly advanced their criminal knowledge in prison. Consider looking for such violent convictions in the last ten to fifteen years, or less if they were first offenders who were granted lenient sentences. They no doubt talk a good game to a sentencing judge and/or a parole board."

Letty's eyes wandered up and to her right, accessing some imaginative profiler database within the recesses of her mind. "This type favors knives over firearms. Their encounters will be up close and brutal—they'd think guns are for pussies. Also, the vic was petite, slender, I think their type. I'd guess they only use raw physical strength to subdue their vics."

Sam's thoughts swirled amid all this speculation. He was a hard evidence guy. But this last bit about them being convicted felons for assault and rape might prove useful. *She's sure getting inside these assholes' heads, if there really are two perps. Even if she's only ten percent right, more 'n I got now. Two perps, not one? She's good. Mary Bishop is—was?—petite and slender, too.*

Letty's eyes closed as she stood leaning on the front left fender of Sam's Bronco. They still fanned out several photos on the hood. She rearranged them, then held one in her left hand, the sheaf of papers comprising the bulk of the case file now in her right. Not looking at any of it at the moment. She was a million miles away. She winced, now muttering almost under her breath. Sam leaned in close to hear what she was saying. "She can't remember. Too painful. This attractive and muscular young girl is used to being in control, even at sixteen, almost seventeen. They took that from her. She can't face it. But something else, too."

"Like what?"

"I don't know. The raw chunk out of her scalp. That bothers me—beyond the obvious reasons. From the girl's perspective, that's a visceral reminder. Something she can touch. That reminder will stay with her. As if at least one of these animals is right behind her with a knife, all the time, for the rest of her life, ready to take another chunk of hair and scalp. I gotta do some more research on this." She shook her head as if to reset her thinking to start fresh.

Sam was now impressed. He never spotted any of this stuff from looking at the girl's photos and case file. This was one impressive young woman. And she didn't insist on being called *Special Agent*. He liked that. She was a pro, but not full of herself. And she wasn't done yet. She misinterpreted the frown on his face.

"Look, Sam, I'll write this up. But my job is to think like a criminal. So, we understand a little of *why* he or she does what they do. But also to help identify *who* they are, *what* they'll do next, and *where* they might do it so we catch the slimy fucks. You feel me?"

"Hey, I get it. What else?" Then her expression changed. She was clearly used to skepticism in the face of her analyses, a relatively new science within the Bureau and law enforcement.

Letty continued. "Okay, then. By the numbers, this sort of criminal comes from a dysfunctional blue-collar family or neighborhood. Escaped from home at an early age, maybe? Let's assume for the moment we *are* looking for two young men. Neither will be handsome. They're both unattractive, unappreciated, and the only way to gain affection from women is to take it, or to pay for it. And Sam?"

"Yeah?" He sensed she had saved the best for last. A silent forehead-wrinkling stare. "What, already!"

"I've seen this *exact* M.O. Four weeks ago, in fact. Up in Maine. One of the primary reasons the Bureau is crashing your party, now, in addition to the Currant kidnapping."

"*What?* You're just now telling me this?"

"I wanted to be sure after being here, seeing the file, and talking with you—eye-to-eye. I was going to wait until after I interviewed the girl. But yes, there is no doubt. Josephine Currant—Josie—is at least victim number two of these monsters. Geraldine Boettcher, a twenty-four-year-old fitness trainer, was beaten, raped repeatedly, and found dead within five hundred feet of the AT on July 5th. M.E. figures she'd been dead two weeks. But we had nothing to connect this to until Josie's case."

Sam was pissed. Felt as if this *special agent* had been holding out on him. But he supposed her approach made sense. Now his mind raged with a shitload of questions.

"Okay, so when you say the same identical M.O., did that include a chunk out of this Geraldine's scalp, too?"

"Yup. Same crew. Down to a tee. Same tape abrasions and bruise patterns, beer sprayed into the vaginal tract, victim left for dead in an obscure location near the AT, although *she* didn't survive. Exposure and dehydration. Dead approximately two weeks when discovered by a team of lumberjacks up near a town called Rangely."

"*Son-of-a-bitch!* Okay, so we got a team of serial rapists-slash-killers to hunt down and fuck over real bad."

"It seems these perps seek random targets of opportunity. But these guys look to be specifically targeting AT through-hikers, or in Josie's case, someone hiking near the trail. On impulse? That is a very specific flavor of psychopathy."

Sam thought back to Doctor Mary Bishop's disappearance, now fearing the worst, that she, too, had fallen prey to these maniacs. Ironic that Grant, Mary's husband, was an authority on aberrant psychology. Sam's expression turned rock hard. He glared at Letty. "What else about these motherfu— these... perps?"

"Sam, this type of criminal exhibits a near-total lack of remorse or guilt. In this case, one more than the other. They're short-tempered with poor impulse control, they're promiscuous, and will have a long history of behavioral problems. I'm thinking they were juvenile delinquents who both exhibited chronic self-esteem issues *and* a grandiose sense of self-worth by artificially compensating. It is almost certain, based on what I've seen in the file, they work jobs that require minimum education and a high degree of raw physical strength. That is also consistent with felons who have served time. For most, staying fit is a matter of survival in prison."

"So, two strong, young, crazed felons who come from a messed-up childhood and think more with their little heads than their slightly less-little heads?"

"Essentially, yes." Letty smiled at Sam's characterization.

# 34

S am sat in his Glenville office. The late morning sun poured through the small twin windows on the building's south side. Resembled a cabin on the outside, and a small multi-desk office inside. Dust motes hung in the brilliant beams of sunlight, rendering them visible. Felt nice. But it still provided insufficient light for office work. Their desk lights burned a helpful incandescent yellow. Agent Mather sat off to his right, placing her in profile at Frank Murdock's old desk—that of his deceased partner. She gazed at the screen of Frank's old computer and spoke softly on the phone with her SAC in Boston. He loved seeing someone at his old partner's desk again, especially someone as full of spunk as this Letty Mather.

Sam jumped when his own phone's jangling broke his daydream. It was Lieutenant Stanfield from CPAC, the Massachusetts State Police Office of Crime Prevention and Control. Lt. Stanfield's MSP unit was assigned to the District Attorney's office to investigate major crimes in Berkshire county. After a brief exchange of pleasantries, the LT got right down to business.

"Sam, sorry to say we have nothing new on the Bishop case, but we got a kidnap survivor. Pretty awful shape. A sixteen-year-old girl named Josie Currant. After searching for a crime scene in this case we're calling a kidnapping, rape, *and* attempted murder, we found nothing up on October Mountain after she showed up on her own out on East New Lenox Road. Even tracking dogs caught the trail given the girl's scent, but it led nowhere. We're spinning our wheels on this one. I sure could use your help, Sam. I'm afraid there's a rapist and possible killer out there, what with that Doctor Bishop missing and now this poor thing. You're one helluva tracker, Sam. Maybe you can talk to this girl, huh?"

"Jeez. Poor kid. Listen, LT, even though kidnapping isn't my specialty—"

"Naw, but tracking is, and you got a way with

people. This kid, Sam, it'll break your heart. Picked her up two weeks ago, even called in the FBI since this *is their* thing. But the kid, well, you'll see. Thing is, without finding where she was held and left for dead, we have nothing. And this kid was so traumatized after wandering down off the mountain, she can't remember anything that helps us to pursue the case. Interested in talking with this girl?"

"Lieutenant, I'm already working this case. I'll be there in two hours. Your office?"

"Oh, great! She's staying at the Lenox Community Hospital in their rehab center. Recovering from her near-death ordeal and seeing therapists, but still nothing."

"I've read the file. A nasty one, LT."

Sam could *sense* the lump rising in the MSP trooper's throat. "Yeah, she's in pretty rough condition, Sam, but she's pulling through, physically, anyway. We're jerking out all the stops, but there's not much more to do until we find where she was held. And Sam, some bastard hacked off a big chunk of her hair, like he was gonna scalp her or something."

Sam's voice sounded brittle. "Pissed me off when I read that." His blood boiled all over again, but he got down to business. "LT, I'll help in any way I can. I have a request, though."

"Name it. We're desperate to get the family some closure."

"I've been working these AT murders and disappearances for about a month. An FBI profiler, a behavioral analyst named Agent Letty Mather, has been a real asset. Plus, having a woman with me at this interview might help this girl remember, or at least be more at ease. Plus, she'll do her own informal psych evaluation at the same time, but from a law enforcement perspective. That might help." Letty looked up from her computer when she heard her name mentioned. She nodded, confirming what Sam promised without asking. He winked back at her.

Sounded like Lieutenant Stanfield sought a pressure relief valve. He snorted. "*What? You* working with a *feeb*? Wonders never cease. Sure. Great idea. Bring her along. I'll call her mother and get permission. Let me reach out to her and I'll let you know when you and your feeb get here."

"Lieutenant, it'd be better if Mom doesn't tag along when we talk with the girl."

"You may have to convince her of that. We've bombarded the shit out of this poor girl over the last two weeks. Claims she's got nothing more. Wait, did you say AT *murders?* Something I don't know?"

"Yeah, well, another case popped in Maine that

preceded this Josie Currant case, and was virtually identical to Currant's, including the missing chunk of scalp and hair. Only that young lady didn't survive. We're thinking there may be others we don't know about yet."

"Oh, shit, Sam."

"Yeah. See you soon."

Twenty minutes later, his Bronco hurled Letty and him toward Lenox. Some monsters were on the loose that needed to be put down. Hard. Sam just hoped he'd get the chance to doing the putting.

# 35

At 1:00 PM that afternoon. they met at the Lenox Community Hospital's rehab center. Sam knew MSP Lieutenant Roy Stanfield to be a straight shooter. "Hey Roy, the family?"

"Yup, a nineteen-year-old sister, Janet, and their thirty-eight-year-old mother named Maeve Currant. They're from Lenox. They're here, too. The father is driving back from a business trip to Ohio. He works for GE."

"Roy, I'd like to chat with them first, just to observe their dynamic."

"No sweat. I hauled them out of the private conference room where Josie is waiting to talk with you. We have Mom and Sister in another lounge for you down the hall."

They walked seventy feet and around two corners to meet Janet, Josie's older sister, who seemed ridden with guilt. Sam introduced Letty and himself. The victim's mother, Maeve, kept hugging Janet while Sam interviewed them. Their heads hung low, forehead to forehead. Letty listened. The only thing the mother talked about was returning to her defiled daughter's side. The two of them had put their own lives on hold since. But Maeve said she wanted to help if it would give them some closure. Janet was sullen, not very responsive, in her own little world. Said Josie had just gone out for a run that day and hadn't returned. Even two weeks downrange of the attack, these two were inconsolable.

This all hit Sam hard. He envisioned how losing Brian would affect him. But that didn't help. "Mrs. Currant, we're gonna do everything possible to catch the monster who attacked your daughter." He didn't bother mentioning Josie was likely attacked by *two* monsters. "But I need your help right now. Letty here and I need to talk with Josie alone. Okay?" The woman looked confused, but true to her word, she said, "Okay, I guess."

. . .

Five minutes later, Sam, Letty and Josie met in a smaller conference room in the rehab center where Josie waited. Three CPAC troopers also in the room included Lt. Stanfield and one of his uniformed female troopers, along with another mountain of a man in a trooper uniform. Looked like a professional wrestler—intimidating as hell. The female trooper's name tag identified her as Trooper Day. Josie sat in a wheelchair and sipped a Diet Squirt with care through one of those bendable hospital straws. She still nursed her busted lip that had required stitches. It took both hands to move that can from the table in front of her to her mouth, and back down again. She set it aside after a single sip.

Josie's bruises covered most of her visible skin and were finally turning from purple to yellow. But bandages covered much of her arms and legs. Another wrapped around the top of her head and under her chin. She'd spent more than a week in the hospital regaining her strength, still looking frail, before moving into the hospital's rehab wing. But she was young, strong, and resilient. They said she was currently undergoing further evaluation and would be scheduled for surgery to repair the damage to the top of her head. Nothing life-threatening, but the wound was more than superficial, and painful, they said.

After her near-death experience, she looked *so* very frail compared to the junior prom photo supplied by her mother. This once vibrant beautiful bundle of energy was... diminished, but not for life, if she was lucky. The two troopers with Lt. Stanfield did a double-take at Sam's and Letty's casual attire who looked at one another and nodded. Sam whispered to Lt. Stanfield. A smirk blossomed on the big man's face, but he nodded. Stanfield gave a small hand signal down low to the male trooper and he took his leave quietly. Lieutenant Stanfield and Trooper Day remained, but only as silent observers from the far side of the room.

As they had agreed, so as to set Josie's tortured mind at ease, Sam wore jeans, sneakers, and an old red and black flannel shirt that had seen better days. Only his badge hanging from his belt identified him as a cop. Letty looked equally casual in a gray sweatshirt emblazoned with "Nantucket" on the front, tight jeans and hiking boots. As Sam had requested.

Sam introduced Letty and himself, along with their jobs—first names only. More familiar. Letty took Sam's cue and offered Josie a glass of water. She accepted. A good start. Sam said, "Josie, they told us what happened to you. We're so very sorry. You've been through an awful lot. No one should have to endure what you did. But your courage and strength got you back. We know that you're still struggling, but we *will* bring the people who did this awful thing to justice. That's what we do, but we can't do it without you."

Silence. Five seconds, ten. Then, she nodded a tiny acknowledgment, still lost in her fears, before she spoke in a hoarse whisper, as if she feared being overheard. Through a bruised mouth with one front tooth missing, she croaked, "I've told them what little I remember."

"I realize that, Josie, but I'm wondering if you're up for a brief ride, just you, me, and Miss Letty here?" Letty added, "Josie, we'd not ask this if it wasn't important. And we'd totally understand if you said no."

"Um, I don't know. Where?"

Sam said, "Back up that mountain a way."

Lt. Stanfield looked at Sam and added in a calm tone from across the room, "We've already taken her up to Camp Eagle. She recognized nothing."

Sam persisted. He leaned forward, rested his elbows on his knees, and folded his hands. "Can we please try, Josie? Get you out of here for a nice ride in the fresh air. If you get scared or uncomfortable, we'll bring you right back, okay?" Josie's eyes were cast downward, but she glanced toward Letty who offered her a tiny nod.

"Okay, but if I start to feel weird, you'll bring me right back?"

Sam said, "Absolutely," and he meant it. Letty nodded.

"Okay then, I'll try."

Letty reached out to squeeze Josie's hand. It was a risk, but Josie didn't pull away. "You're a brave young woman and we will make sure we take good care of you." The girl now seemed resigned to the task, but continued shaking. Looked like she was still balanced on the very edge of a dangerous emotional precipice. No wonder they were keeping her here for the time being.

Sam drove his green Bronco. Letty and Josie sat in the back seat. Josie insisted that the windows remain rolled down. As they drove up the bumpy mountain road near the trailhead where Sam thought she might have come, Josie seemed reassured by their company. Sam kept the conversation light, with only a few general questions. The tough stuff would come next.

# 36

The steep and twisting road up the mountain sliced through a variety of flora and fauna in the mid-afternoon sunlight. As they passed a large patch of tall blackberry bushes, Sam followed the girl's eyes in the rearview mirror. Josie jerked her gaze away from that side of the road. *She's remembering how she got at least some of those deep lacerations on her arms and legs. Good.* Blackberry bushes protect themselves with wicked thorns. They rip your clothes to shreds. She had been dazed and naked, running through them in the dark. By the sheer number of bandages and what her doctor had told them, she got ripped up quite badly. *No wonder she's looking away, poor kid.*

After twenty minutes of rather slow driving on the rough road, not much more than a mountain trail, they arrived at a place called Camp Eagle. A marked State Police cruiser had followed them up. Everyone crawled out of the two vehicles. Josie shivered. Sam reached for her left upper arm. Letty did the same on her right. When Letty saw the girl's eyes widen as she pulled away, just a little—more like a spasm—she whispered to Josie, "In case you trip or fall, sweetie, as you're still pretty weak. That'll pass."

Sam muttered to no one in particular. "Sure is beautiful up here. That little pond brings a kind of serenity to this place."

Josie looked up at Sam. Her expression hinted that he demonstrated a knack for saying the wrong thing at the wrong time. But her mouth said, "The troopers brought me up here, and nothing looked familiar. Still doesn't."

"That's okay, Josie. But remember, you didn't come up the road, since you came up by that trail over there. Said they carried you and you were unconscious. So, no worries about that part because you weren't able to see it." Sam took a breath. "What was the first thing you remember when you regained consciousness?"

"Tied to a tree by this really big guy and he had a friend who was almost as big."

"Two men." He nodded his appreciation toward Letty. "Big how? Tall, fat, muscular....?"

Lt. Stanfield looked surprised. New information!

"Not so tall, but strong, like bodybuilders."

Letty said, "That's really good, Josie. Do you remember what they talked about?"

"No, I don't remember. So scared."

"Afterward, what were they doing or what did they do?" asked Letty.

"Both of them... peed all over me," her lower lip quivered up and down. Josie teared up, barely able to continue. Stumbled, but they both caught her. They stopped walking so Josie could focus. "They were drunk, and started throwing wet grass and mud at me, laughing and snorting. I didn't want to think anymore, Sam. I just closed my eyes and pretended I was dead...."

---

Letty caught that Josie called Sam by his first name. Familiarity, a little trust building. Sam said he was convinced they were close to the crime scene, but couldn't put his finger on the right next question, the one that nobody had yet asked. Everyone stopped talking as they stood there, looking around.

Lt. Stanfield looked at Sam with a puckered brow, an expression that seemed to say, "So, are we done here?" Sam caught that, but ignored him. That's when a light bulb popped for him. "Josie, do you remember what color the mud was?" Both the LT and Letty looked at Sam as if to say, *what?*

Josie shut her eyes tight, lowered her head, and clenched her fists. It was like she now didn't want to disappoint her new friend, Sam. He said, "Take your time, Josie. Try hard to visualize. You said yourself you didn't want to look *anymore,* which means you *did look* at some point and *did observe something*, didn't you?" He kept his voice low and smooth. All of a sudden, she popped open her eyes, as much as the residual bruising allowed. She almost smiled—her busted lip stopped her with a painful wince as the stitches stretched—but it was still clear she experienced a minor victory. With excitement now in her voice, "The mud was very dark, almost black, and real slippery."

"Excellent, Josie. I think that's all we need for now. We're going to take you back to your mom and sister right away. Sorry this was so difficult for you. But you were a huge help today. Thank you. We'll stop in on you from time to time to see how you're doing and also to let you know of any more stuff we find out." He turned his attention to Lt. Stanfield. "Roy, would you have one of your troopers take Josie home, please?" The LT nodded to Trooper Day. She walked over and gently touched Josie's arm. Sam turned her way. "Thanks, Trooper Day. Take good care of her." He winked at Josie, who returned a small smile until she winced again at stretching her broken lip. Trooper Day nodded to Sam, they turned, and headed for her cruiser.

Lt. Stanfield said, "Okay, Sam, what gives?"

"Come with me, Roy." The other huge trooper that rode with Day followed them. The foursome walked around to the backside of the small three-acre pond off to their left. They entered the dense woods near the pond. About two hundred circuitous yards later, the woods thinned. A small clearing came into view. Sam swiveled a playful gaze, first at Lt. Stanfield, then at Letty. "There's your crime scene, Roy." They strolled into that clearing that was less than fifty feet across, mindful not to disturb what they saw. Strewn on the ground were candy wrappers, a dozen beer cans, and assorted trash that was most certainly laden with fingerprints and DNA. Letty and the LT stared at Sam in amazement. Before they could ask, he said. "Josie described dark, almost black mud that was "real slippery." I knew there was a peat bog back here—dark mud, almost black, and kinda slimy. Until then, I wasn't asking the right question."

Lt. Stanfield said with a big grin on his face, "Excellent, EPO Travis." He slapped Sam on the back. "I'll get our crime scene techs all over this place within the hour. Did it again, Sam. You never disappoint. I'll just say you'd have made one hell of a trooper, son." He then grabbed the side of Sam's right shoulder and vigorously shook his hand with the other. Sam grinned back and said, "LT, please let me know what you come up with so we can match it to our other vics. We're pretty sure it's the same guys." With that, they hiked away with the big trooper left behind to keep the scene secure until the techs arrived.

Letty turned to Sam, now sitting in his Bronco and stared. Sam sensed her looking at him with his peripheral vision. He said, "What?" without turning his eyes away from the windshield, even though they weren't moving yet.

Letty purred, tongue in cheek, "Very nice, Sam Travis. You could almost be an average FBI agent! I heard you just collared a crooked federal agent *and* helped catch a corrupt AUSA? It would seem you are on a roll, EPO Travis."

They both busted out in a hearty laugh they sorely needed.

Then Sam fell silent. So did Letty. He muttered through gritted teeth, "Now we got two more mongrels to put down."

# 37

The same memories plagued the two young men as if they were of a single mind. Right out of high school, Liam and Conor had played malicious pranks on common folk for a while. Just for the excitement of it. Blew up mailboxes with M-80s, punctured tires, threw rocks from the road at random house windows.... Seemed silly, now.

But on a very particular night back in 1979, one humiliating memory plagued Liam, one from which he never shook loose. Not even all these years later. Fueled his rage, almost like no other, especially toward women—all women. What happened that night almost a decade earlier would not only define both of their lives, it might also be the source of something resembling regret—a devastating rarity for Liam. He remembered that night and cringed....

---

Conor and Liam had hungered for something to appease the hormonal rage that burned within both of them that summer of 1979. They became obsessed over shedding their virginity, like a snake shedding its skin. Karamusell had a small red-light district. Both boys vowed to spend a hundred dollars each, a fortune, on a whore to end this virginity shit. Few streetlights still burned on Palmer Street, those not blown to hell with pellet guns. The girls liked the not-so-well-lit neighborhood for their brand of work. Their pimps and muscle were always near, but seldom seen.

Liam found two older women working the street who'd take their money to service this pair of young studs. The whores looked fine with their heavy make-up in the bad light. They took the boys upstairs to a small, grungy walk-up that smelled bad. "It's a whorehouse, not a hotel," Liam told Conor after seeing his disdain for the place.

The older one said, "Money up front, boys."

Disrobed, they stood naked in front of these middle-aged women who both lay side by side on the solitary bed in the room with only a little netting now covering their bodies. Seeing their large breasts and pubic hair drove Liam into a frenzy. The single candle in the dreary little room almost rendered their purple stretch marks, chicken skin and wrinkles invisible. The older woman, sporting bright red hair sure to be a wig, fondled Liam. Totally erect and ready to burst, Liam entered her. He lasted two strokes before exploding. He roared like a lion. The woman pulled away in that instant. Conor experienced the same right next to him with the other woman. Red said, "Okay, you both came. We're done for tonight unless you have more green to stay longer."

At first, this confused Liam. "I thought I paid for the whole night!"

"For a hundred bucks? Not hardly, muscleman. You paid for one shot and you got it. That's it, sonny." Conor remained confused.

"*No way!* That didn't even take a minute. You gotta give me more."

"Sorry, honey, those are the rules. They're posted on that sheet of paper on the wall over there. Be a nice boy now and come visit Viviah again. Only jerk off first, so you last a little longer." And then she laughed. Furious, Liam backhanded her. She screamed.

Heavy footsteps on the stairs preceded two enforcers bursting through the door. They made quick work of Liam. Both boys left the whorehouse bruised and deflated. And worse, more angry that their egos had been shattered. It was still early. They cruised and cursed and drank. They got drunk on more talk of violence, and how badly they were treated. "Damn women. Hate 'em." Their vitriol against women—all women—escalated that night. They needed to feed the beast, a primal imperative that would last the rest of their lives.

Later that same Wednesday night back in June of 1979, they'd pick up Ginny Swanson, the girl that sent them to prison. A night to remember... for two *very* different reasons.

# 38

---

Ginny Swanson often relived the night Liam and Conor attacked her nine years earlier, like it was hours ago, not years. Tonight was no exception. She'd never look at a man without fear ever again. Ginny had just awakened from the same nightmare she'd suffered through every night since that awful night. In this same horrific dream, she looked down at herself as she stumbled around, like that night, before finding a road and her savior....

---

June 13, 1979

. . .

Mrs. Martha Eldrich, a gentle sixty-three-year-old widow, made her way to work at the twenty-four-hour diner on County Road 4 that night. The pouring rain reduced visibility to worse than awful, so she drove with great care on the curvy two-lane road. Martha prided herself on being a careful driver. Now, with the onset of macular degeneration, she hated driving at night, but a girl had to earn a living. Plus, she rather enjoyed being a waitress at the County Line diner. Got her out of her double-wide to mingle with real folks. Well, folks who prowled the night, anyway. She worked third shift—from eleven PM til the butt crack of dawn. Suited her crummy sleeping habits just fine.

Less than five miles from the diner, Martha thought she saw something in the middle of the road. Her too-old wipers gone brittle swiped as fast as they were able. She slowed down further. That's when it happened. She slammed on her brakes. Her car slid sideways. She had almost hit what looked like a small deer. *Is that a naked, barefoot girl, half stumbling, half crawling down the center of the road?* Not sure if she could trust her eyes, until the girl collapsed to the asphalt, no longer moving, less than ten feet from Martha's front passenger door.

It took every bit of Martha's strength to drag the tiny girl's mostly dead weight into her back seat. The girl regained semi-consciousness as she lay across the seat of Martha's old Ford Grenada. "What's your name, honey?" Nothing. "Well, I'm gonna get you to the hospital, so you rest, dearie, okay?" Only a weak nod.

Martha did a U-turn on the narrow two-lane road and headed back toward Harrington. Drove as fast as she dared, with frequent glances over her shoulder at the pitiable sight. Adjusted her rearview mirror to monitor the girl without taking her sore eyes off the road, what with all the flaring and halos around every light. *Darned old eyes!* Pulled up to the emergency room entrance of the Harrington General Hospital sixteen miles from where she'd almost hit this poor girl. She wanted to wait around, but she had a shift to work. Left her name and phone number with the ER admissions clerk and went to work. Hated leaving the poor thing, but a girl's gotta earn a living.

---

The ER admissions clerk called the local police. Their small-town rape crisis team, led by a female officer, arrived fifteen minutes later. The attending

ER physician made them wait until the girl was conscious and was able to speak. It took a sedative, some time, an IV for rehydration, and a little conversation to get her to that point. Before interviewing the girl, however, the officer talked with the attending. Confirmed the girl suffered not only a brutal battering, but was also the victim of violent and repetitive sexual abuse. The attending had ordered a rape kit, and was charting the results, with more to come. But she wanted to get as much documented as possible before the police crisis team arrived. The lead officer nodded her thanks and asked to talk with the victim.

Entered the room and balked at the site. She'd seen more than her share of rape victims after three years on the team, but this poor girl was worse than any she'd seen.

"Miss, my name is Officer Troy. Can you tell me your name? Miss?"

"Um, Ginny."

"Hi, Ginny. Who did this to you?"

"Two boys."

"Do you know them?"

"Uh-huh. Liam Sullivan and his friend. I think his name is Conor."

"How do you know them, Ginny?"

"High school."

"Here in Harrington?"

"Karamusell."

---

Ginny was never the same after that night nine years ago, even though her attackers had gone to prison. At least *they'd* get out of *their* prison eventually, maybe already were. Wished with all her heart she could say the same.

# 39

The FBI convened an emergency task force that was to meet at one of their locations on the coast. Their theory? The location was secure and equally accessible by all agencies involved. Almost. Except for the EPOs and Massachusetts State Police coming from the far western part of the state, where the subject crimes of this task force took place. A bulletin from MSP headquarters directed to the Mass Turnpike Barracks across the state, from Boston to the New York border, would shorten the trip's elapsed time. The bulletin read:

*"Be advised that three unmarked MSP cruisers will be in formation traveling in the high-speed lane from approximately 0800 to 1000 hours. DO NOT STOP OR ENGAGE. Repeat: DO NOT STOP OR ENGAGE. All courtesies of the road to be extended. Assist or escort if possible." - Auth: Lt. Col. John Spellacy, MSP HQ.*

Lt. O'Neill and EPO Travis were in one black unmarked Ford LTD Crown Victoria, a five-liter, 302 cubic-inch V8 with the cop package. These LTDs were beasts. They met two Dana barracks MSP troopers outside their cruisers at the entrance to the turnpike at 8 AM. After a brief conversation with the troopers, O'Neill returned to his vehicle. Said to Travis "This will be the fastest trip on the 'pike you'll ever experience." Travis smiled and said, "Okay, boss, hit it." They also cleared Route 93 that intersected the pike. The three cruisers made the hundred-sixty-miles in an hour-ten.

A ten-foot chain-link fence topped with razor wire guarded a nondescript warehouse at the designated address in Newburyport north of Boston. One vehicle after another approached its gate mid-morning. FBI vehicles entered a code and passed through as it opened and closed behind each sedan or SUV. Vehicles from all other agencies displayed their credentials, got checked off a list and were admitted by the gate's armed guard. His partner watched from behind what they presumed to be bullet-resistant glass. They weren't wrong.

The sign on the battleship-gray building read Kendale Industries Limited. To a select few within the FBI, they knew this as one of the Bureau's *black sites*. To Sam, this entire set-up seemed excessive, but then the federal budget left any state budget in the dust. A whole new level.

Once past yet another security barrier inside the fence, entry keypads on the building required codes established just for today's meeting. This was managed by yet another armed guard who acknowledged the officers with a wordless nod. Inside, this building looked less like a warehouse, and more like an office complex, at least the parts they observed. Sam and his boss were escorted. Led through a small maze of rooms and offices, most of which contained computers and bright-blinking modems moving data, but very few people.

They arrived at the meeting's location—a third-floor conference room—five minutes later. They had lined its mammoth table with yellow legal pads, all brand new, with three pens resting on each. A dark projector sat poised for action. Sam thought, *Man, a whole different vibe when you have an unlimited budget.*

Travis and O'Neill met Letty's boss and task force commander, Special Agent-in-Charge Winston Daniels, up from the FBI Behavioral Analysis Unit (BAU) at Quantico, Virginia, part of the Bureau's National Center for the Analysis of Violent Crime. That meant the feds were taking this case *very* seriously. Letty was not here, however.

There were a couple of men from the US Fish and Wildlife Service—one of whom looked to be in charge, and the other likely a field officer. Same with the Massachusetts State Police, Maine's Warden Service and New Hampshire Fish and Game. Including Sam and Paul O'Neill representing the Massachusetts Environmental Police, the room bristled with a dozen serious law enforcement types. They all knew they needed a comprehensive cross-agency plan to stop the spree perpetrated by this pair of serial rapists and killers. *Nice digs, this FBI "site." Deep pockets.*

# 40

The meeting began when Letty's boss sat down at the head of the table without saying a word—without question, the man in charge. All eyes turned toward him, everyone fell silent and took a seat. This was to be an FBI operation, overall. Sam wasn't much for meetings, but recognized its importance with the lousy press *every* law enforcement agency was getting over this case, not to mention the victims were piling up, and the *very* public stink Doctor Grant Bishop was slinging to every media outlet who would listen to the story of his missing wife, Mary.

Once SAC Daniels finished his introductory

remarks, he invited everyone around the table to introduce themselves. He then clicked a remote in front of him. The projector and its fan whirred to life. On the wall behind him appeared a large topo-graphical map illustrating locations of where each victim had been found or the last known position of anyone who recently went missing on or near the Appalachian Trail. He then stood, moved to the middle of the table's long side and hunched over a large paper map that duplicated what was on the screen. Everyone seated at the table also stood and peered at the paper map. Cops still liked paper. He pointed to each of three marked and labeled loca-tions to ensure the entire task force was on the same page:

- A red circle in grease pencil depicted the body recovery site of Geraldine Boettcher's body in Maine, labeled Body #1,
- An orange circle for survivor, Josie Currant in Massachusetts, labeled "Survivor #2"; and,
- A yellow circle for the last known position of Doctor Mary Bishop, also in Massachusetts, labeled "Missing, #3?"

They had marked watering holes (W) and shelters (S) along the AT from Maine to the border between Western Massachusetts and Connecticut. Other geographical bullet points were annotated around the map's periphery, such as distance to nearest law enforcement, type-of-vehicle access, and nearest air support. Staffers had spent serious time with this map in preparation for this meeting. *Yup, deep pockets,* Sam thought, again.

The feds thought the shelters should be staked out. Sam disagreed and said so. "All due respect, shelters will be hit or miss. But watering holes? Water is too heavy to transport on foot in bulk. So, hikers *always* stop at watering holes. Like in the wilds of Africa where predators stake out water holes. But here, these two-legged predators are stalking their prey."

It appeared they had taken on an insurmountable surveillance task. Given their working assumptions that the perps would strike next either in Maine or Massachusetts, but not knowing where, they would need coverage from the trail's northern end in Maine at Baxter Peak on Mount Katahdin to the length of trail ending at the Massachusetts-Connecticut line. That covered damn-near six hundred miles. Seemed an impossible task.

So, based on probability and behavioral analyses, they decided to focus on four of the most likely spots the perps might strike next. Most likely were specific watering holes near the AT, according to the profilers at FBI's BAU and the best intelligence information from all agencies: two in Maine, one in New Hampshire, and one in Massachusetts. If necessary, they'd then change their focus beyond those to additional targets as manpower allowed, or God forbid, as additional victims further defined a more predictable pattern. Not ideal, but it was a start. They had a plan.

SAC Daniels asked, "Lieutenant O'Neill, how is your EPO command positioned for support of this plan?"

"Sir, we are a small organization and spread thin. It's been a rough few months. Captain Jamison is still in the hospital, and we're short one EPO who was murdered several months ago. We haven't been able to replace him yet. Budget issues complicate matters."

Sam piped up. "Sir, I'd suggest that our EPO team *could* cover the selected location in Massachusetts for a three-day vigil. I know that area like the back of my hand. Longer than three days nonstop in the woods just isn't optimal for any team." SAC Daniels agreed and moved on.

O'Neill read Travis like a book. He whispered,

"Okay, Sam, I can see you're really getting invested in this case. Remember, a seasoned investigator knows that too much empathizing with victims will also victimize the investigator."

"Yeah, I know. You shoulda seen that Josie kid. But for this op, boss, here's the rub. We're gonna need an attractive young woman for bait. The only woman I can think of who is attractive *but* strong *and* trained for such a risky job is FBI—Special Agent Letty Mather. If you agree, Paul, I think she'd go for this. Could we get her on assignment? Unlike the feds here, I'm thinking of this as more of a sting operation than a surveillance gig."

Sam's idea made Paul nervous. So many things could go wrong. "I get it. Yes, I'll feel out her boss. See what he says." He side-nodded toward SAC Daniels. "You're right, we can't turn this into a federal circus, or our perps won't come within a hundred miles of your watering hole *or any shelter.*"

SAC Daniels kept the meeting on point, allowing only concise discussions to resolve points of contention. They had agreed to a plan in less than two hours. This plan included which organization would handle each assignment and the number of personnel to be deployed, with additional assets in reserve. Also, the plan outlined who would support them and precisely where they were to be positioned in case an extensive ground search would be required. These supply and support facilities included air support, medical, and transportation (over-the-road, off-road, or all-terrain vehicles). This plan also enabled appropriate resources to respond to any of the four initial sites selected quickly and efficiently.

Impressive, but way over-designed in Sam's mind. Daniels's staffers issued a pair of satellite phones to each of the four designated surveillance teams, along with a cheat sheet of all their phone numbers to each team leader.

One team from one agency would surveil each site rather than throwing people from different agencies together. But two undercover FBI agents nearby each site would provide secondary support. So, they designated each of their four initial targets to one agency as primary, comprising at least three state-level officers assigned to each watering hole.

The FBI would also be the primary and take up station at Frenchman's Hole in Maine, deemed the most probable next target. The Maine Warden Service would set up at Garfield Brook, Maine as primary, with another site manned by New Hampshire Fish and Game at Little River Falls in New Hampshire. And finally, Massachusetts Environmental Police would take the least likely watering hole at Upper Goose Pond in Massachusetts. Sam's input weighed heavily in the choice of this spot. Said he had a feeling. The feds who knew of Sam did not roll their eyes. This guy had a good track record following his gut. As with the other three sites, two FBI undercover agents would hang back at an AT shelter called Smith's Cabin less than two-hundred yards from Sam's watering hole.

---

Captain Jamison still recuperated at Berkshire Medical. He claimed he was being held hostage. The doctors said he was fine, but needed to rest another day or so. Further, FBI profiler Letty Mather agreed to accompany EPO Travis to the Upper Goose Pond stake-out to make up for their personnel shortage. With her SAC's blessing, of course. Their short but successful history of working together helped. Lieutenant O'Neill committed to stand by at a nearby ranger station in addition to the two FBI agents at

Smith's Cabin. The entire task force orchestrated a three-day and three-night vigil to begin in forty-eight hours. After this initial deployment, they'd checkpoint via a conference call to discuss next steps as might be required. None really expected results from this first outing. None except Sam Travis.

# 41

Two days later, a Sunday, EPO rookie Al Stukowski had been called over from his new post in Cheshire. He dropped Agent Mather and EPO Travis at the trailhead to the AT's Upper Goose Pond access point. With full packs, Letty and Sam hiked into their assigned area, the one Sam had recommended to the task force. The two FBI agents assigned to support that surveillance site had their own ride and met Sam and Letty at the trailhead. From there, Sam and Letty headed to the watering hole, the two agents to the nearby cabin, and Lieutenant O'Neill to the nearest ranger station a mile away. All were to check in via their sat phones every four hours or if anything popped.

On the ride up to their designated stake-out, Sam now worried. "How do you feel about being bait, Special Agent Mather?" They were way past formal titles, but Sam was making a point.

"Officer Travis, I think you're on to a scenario with a reasonable expectation of success. Yes, I'm happy to be the bait in your little field op."

"But—?"

"Don't worry. I've already sold this as a *profiling side-op* to support the main case. After all, I'm *just* a profiler in the field agents' eyes." Sam couldn't miss the angst in her voice that apparently made her a bit of a fifth wheel among most field agents' minds. Also, a woman in a man's world. He liked her more and more. "But we're under a helluva lot of pressure to catch these guys. If they come a sniffing, this'll work, Sam. Thanks for including me."

"My boss still thinks this whole idea presents too much risk."

"I'm a big girl with a big gun and a bigger attitude."

*Yeah, I like this woman, even if she **is** a feeb.*

# 42

Rather than staking out the watering hole proper, Sam and Letty had agreed to improvise on the ride up to the trail-head. They'd set an irresistible trap to entice Liam Sullivan and Conor Juszynska, assuming they were in the area. The mountainous trail leading to the lake was steep and rugged. Mather impressed Travis with her stamina and considerable climbing skills.

Once at "the pond," they scouted it out. The watering hole—a natural cold-water spring that Sam had visited by boat just three weeks earlier—was where hikers trafficked down off the nearby AT to fetch water. It was on the AT hiker's map. The spring was actually in the center of a small peninsula that jutted out into the rather large pond, a euphemism for this lake. Campers used this spot because of the cool, alluring blue-green water with crystal clarity. The peninsula wasn't large—less than seventy-five feet wide and about a hundred feet long. Perfect. Letty wore a tank top, shorts, hiking socks under some serious boots, and pitched her tent fifty feet off the well-trodden trail to the water's edge. She was well-armed, appeared at ease, and unrolled two thin but warm blankets from her pack to counter the cool Berkshire nights.

They already had plenty of evidence tying these assholes to earlier attacks, resulting in at least two rapes, one homicide and one attempted murder, so far. But Sam wanted to not only catch them, he wanted to catch them in the act if they showed up. He needed them to attack Letty. How far was he willing to let it go before intervening? She wanted the same thing—to nail these bastards in the act. *Demanded* that Sam not intervene until they had taken her down, and... she only said, "Get them with the goods in hand, Sam. Get them with the goods." *The girl's got balls, alright.*

Travis planted a trio of well-camouflaged wireless trail cams in the trees well above shoulder height using a small four-foot fold-up ladder he'd had strapped to his backpack on the hike in. He placed two cams on the trail that led onto the peninsula, and one overlooking the lake in case Sullivan and Juszynska boated in. The cams were infrared-capable with proximity alerts to detect motion and should present a clear image even in near-total darkness. They called the pair of agents at the nearby cabin and O'Neill at the ranger station with the sat phones borrowed from the feds. Nothing else worked out here except walkies and they were just too noisy. And their range was insufficient in the mountainous terrain. All assets were now on site, but Sam had been adamant about only him and Letty at the watering hole. O'Neill objected, but he trusted Sam and acquiesced. Even though others felt this location was least likely to be the next target, Travis's instincts were pushing him to prepare for action.

---

The sun descended below the tree line by the time Sam completed his hide of hemlock boughs near a large red oak fifty feet south of Letty's tent. Once in his hide, he would be invisible, and the two of them would speak little. If anyone came down the footpath onto their little peninsula, the cameras set at fifty-foot intervals on the steep approach trail should alert Travis. After their perps walked past, he'd sneak in behind them. Inside her tent, Letty would play soft new-age music with a small camp lantern glowing.

Now dressed in warmer clothes, she prepared her placement of tactical assets. She'd keep her Bureau-issued 9mm Glock 19 service weapon at the ready as well as a sheathed razor-sharp five-inch double-edged fighting knife. Two flashlights, an expandable bone-snapping baton, and pepper spray completed her arsenal.

Sam enjoyed watching Letty. There was a crisp efficiency in her every movement, and she was no stranger to roughing it. *Must do a lot of camping. Looks like she's even enjoying herself. But she's gotta have a history. There's a... damaged intensity... about her.* Letty seemed a natural for field work even though still untested.

In his old hip holster, Sam carried his trusty .357 magnum loaded with six +P (souped-up high-velocity) rounds that boasted six-hundred pounds of muzzle energy traveling at eighteen-hundred feet-per-second. He also packed a five-shot Smith and Wesson .38 snubby, also with +P rounds, plus a few speed-loaders for each. With those speed-loaders, he'd reload either the monster three-five-seven or the versatile little snubby in a second or two. Sam was an expert with both weapons, especially "the beast," the perfect balance between punching power and accuracy.

Night fell. Before they assumed their positions for their vigil after which they'd engage in minimal interaction, they ate and discussed their near-silent communication codes. One click meant "I hear something." Two clicks meant "someone is here." And three clicks signaled "SOS," that is, all hell is breaking loose and I need immediate assistance to stay alive. This would be their only use of the small walkies they'd toted in. They'd tap one, two, or three quick depressions of the push-to-talk button on one unit, which they'd hear on the other unit. Their set-up and plans were complete. Now, they'd wait.

# 43

They intended to take these boys alive, if possible. But given their extraordinary physical strength reported by the prison in Albion, Pennsylvania, they'd need to assume a hand-to-hand victory would be a challenge; although Travis still believed strength alone would not win the day. Almost never did. Sam took a deep breath and let it out slow. "Ready, Letty?"

"Yes, I am, Sam. By the way, I agree with your recommendation. I, too, still feel this is a good place to be."

Sam replied in a low voice that was all business. "Okay, then, leave your lantern on, and soft music.

Service weapon in hand. Sound travels far in these hills, so stay alert."

Letty replied in her husky whisper, "Not my first rodeo, cowboy. Besides, you'll be sleeping like a baby in fifteen minutes."

Sam chuckled under his breath as he looked her in the eye. "Hey, we gotta sleep sooner or later. My trail cams will alert us if anything larger than a possum lumbers in toward us." He shot a glance down at the four-inch monitor in his lap. His cams were reporting in, but no moving targets, and no alerts. "I got your back, Letty. You're a natural for field work." Another smile saw him untangle his legs. He stood, turned, and retreated to his hide. The long night remained uneventful, with nothing more than a couple of raccoons sniffing around the camp-fire for scraps. They were used to getting freebies from campers. Morning came, and every unit checked in via the sat phones with no results at any site. Everyone alternated grabbing cat naps.

Night two. Sam picked Letty's brain from within his hide as she sat nearby. She couldn't see him, anyway. They didn't know if they were watched, as unlikely as that was. He muttered, "Do you think these mongrels are more likely to show up to party during the day or after dark?"

"Well, their psychoses indicate unpredictability.

But now that they're well-practiced and thoughtful about their takedowns, I'm betting they see their prey more vulnerable late in the day or after dark. Plus, it's easier to surprise and disorient a victim if they've been sleeping for a while."

After more trail food and a check-in on one of their phones, they were ready for another long night. Nothing. Same drill next day. Fatigue and boredom were the worst enemies of surveillance. But Sam's gut told him this night would be different.

# 44

Liam said to Conor, "I like Massachusetts. That lady doctor north of here last month on our way down from Maine *was* pretty sweet. Lots of good places to camp down here. Tonight's gonna be another good night if we find another one."

Conor still thought they were pushing their luck, but he did like the party at the end of a hunt. "Where we gonna find one tonight?"

Liam aimed his flashlight at the map he held propped against the wheel of the old truck they'd stolen the night before. "There's a watering hole on this here AT map called Upper Goose Pond. Remote as hell, but popular with the hikers, and I'm bettin' there ain't no roads or telephone service anywhere around. We'll have to hike a ways up a mountain. I seen a picture somewheres, and it looks real good. There's even an AT shelter nearby, but first, we're gonna go off the trail for this hunt, Conor. I got this here tickle in my antenna...."

Now getting more into the spirit, Conor hooted, "Yeah, baby!"

Both Letty and Sam were slumping, drowsy and stiff from the tension, fatigue, and immobility on the downslope of this three-day surveillance op. Both looked forward to hot food and an even hotter shower. But they remained professional. Letty planted her behind on a log less than five feet from Sam's hide. Hadn't seen him more than a glimpse in two days. Still didn't. He took his job seriously. But she recognized *he* could see *her*. Weird. She whispered, "It's so gorgeous and peaceful here. It's hard to fathom it any other way, isn't it, Sam?"

The sun had been casting long shadows for a while, turning the surrounding colors into stunning golds and rich browns. The light now faded fast, along with his remaining energy. They sat in a mutual silence for about ten minutes. She arose and as she started shuffling away toward her tent, she muttered as if talking to herself, "Let's hope it's a quiet night."

Sam whispered, "Agent Mather, I'm hoping we get lucky." He couldn't see her face, but she snorted as if in self-amusement. With so much time alone, Sam sought any distraction. Almost without thinking, he grabbed a tin of camo paint from his tactical vest and slathered a layer on his face, neck and the backs of his hands. If he was invisible before, he'd be a damn ghost now. This old Marine habit hadn't occurred to him in a while. Tonight, it did. No explaining it.

This far from civilization, the sky glowed—zero light pollution. But tonight, a little after 10:00 PM, a cloudy sky obscured the sliver of a moon and every speck of starlight. A few end-of-night embers from Letty's fire provided the dimmest glow from within a rock ring erected by earlier campers. She lit the lantern inside her tent. Sam fidgeted with his pocket knife. Just then, his little four-inch lap monitor beeped and a small red light blinked at him. He jumped. The device's audible alert signal pierced the silence. He muted it. Trail camera one, the farthest away, transmitted a blue-gray night-vision image of a man ascending the trail. Liam Sullivan? Five seconds later, another man carrying a shoulder bag passed cam one. Conor Juszynska? Yup, these were their mutts, alright, and they were coming in—stealthy. God bless wireless trail cams. Sam alerted Letty with two clicks. She acknowledged with two clicks of her own. *Someone is here.*

Moments later, cam two lit up. They headed their way, for sure. If their objective was the pond's watering hole, they'd pass within fifty feet of Letty's tent now glowing from her lantern inside. He could hear her music, too. Now that he was sure, Sam punched the speed-dial on the sat phone. Whispered to Lt. O'Neill standing by at the ranger station a mile away, "Boss, our two boys are headed up this way. Confirming it's Sullivan and Juszynska."

O'Neill responded, "Roger. En route, code three." That meant lights and sirens, at least, to the trailhead down the mountain. In other words, ASAFP.

---

Of course, O'Neill updated his EPO dispatcher. Captain Larry Jamison heard the whole thing on his portable scanner on the table beside his hospital bed. The hospital wasn't all that far from O'Neill's ranger station. He'd glued himself to that device ever since he'd checked himself in. The truth was he didn't feel all that terrible, but wanted to stay close to the action here in Berkshire County, not ninety minutes away at his apartment in Framingham. His doctors didn't object. Now, he dragged his ass out of bed and winced in pain as he yanked on his street clothes. Made his escape and screamed out of the hospital's parking lot in his cruiser—also code three.

Jamison hailed O'Neill on the car's radio to inform him in no uncertain terms he was en route from nearby Berkshire Medical to Travis's location. "Paul, I know where they are, better than you. No time to waste or explain. I've got the lead on this and not a peep out of you. I'll contact the SAC. Got it, Paul?"

"Yes, sir." O'Neill knew better than to argue with his boss, even though he was closer—and in better shape. "I'll monitor the trailhead out of there, so nobody leaves without us knowing about it."

"Good man." Larry jumped on his car phone with SAC Daniels, the task force commander, with the number provided by O'Neill. He was already screaming up the mountain road to Upper Goose Pond's access point at the boat ramp and advised that their suspects were confirmed approaching the

Upper Goose hole. SAC Daniels responded with a crisp, let-there-be-no-doubt tone in his voice, "I'm calling the state barracks. They have troopers ready to roll."

"Roger that. Thanks." And Larry meant it. He feared for Travis and that female FBI agent with him. He'd never been comfortable sending just the two of them out on this stake-out. Even with two FBI agents standing by. But now, there they were. He'd just gotten confirmation from SAC Daniels there indeed were two of his agents at Smith's Cabin less than two hundred yards from Sam's location and they had been alerted, too.

But Sam had been crystal clear. "Keep them back unless we call them." Didn't want to scare their perps into disappearing in these dense woods.

# 45

Liam and Conor were like ghosts in the woods. They'd done this before and knew their way around trails. Travis was pretty quiet himself, a mere ten feet behind them with his .357 out in the low ready position in one hand, and his expanded baton in the other. Pretty clear these mopes had decent night vision. They approached Letty's tent, no doubt expecting an oblivious hiker chick, listening to some fancy chick music and burning a chick lantern like it was a sissy nightlight.

Once they opened the tent flap, Sam planned to take out Liam with a solid blow to the neck with his expandable baton, a vicious weapon. That'd put him down. Then the same for the other mope. He'd need to wail on this guy to incapacitate him. Closed the distance as Liam reached for the closed tent flap's zipper. Sam ignored the shorter one for the moment, still eight feet away, in favor of first putting down the obvious alpha dog. He wound up his baton, swung and *slammed* Liam across the back of his neck with every bit of his strength, which was considerable. That blow would have put any man down. Not Liam. Too much muscle and sinew. He was rocked and wobbled, but did not go down.

Liam turned quickly on a surprised Sam and slapped the baton out of his hand as if punishing a child for playing with a forbidden toy. Sam's right index finger slipped into the trigger guard of his big revolver as he swung it up to aim. But that hand got swatted away, too, although not before the big gun blasted a hole in the dirt near Liam's right foot. Sam cursed himself for not reacting faster. This guy was as quick as he was big. He'd been too cocky.

While deciding how to defend himself from this monster, he yelled to Letty, "Behind you!" He saw through the thin nylon tent's wall, Letty's silhouette turned to fire from inside the tent. But before she got a shot off, the tent collapsed on top of her as Conor launched himself onto the dome tent. By now, Liam had recovered from Sam's attack. The two men squared off. Sam saw crazy in the hulk's eyes. The brute whistled a giant swing toward the side of Sam's head with a hambone fist that missed by less than an inch. He felt the breeze of it. Sam quickly countered with a solid right to Liam's jaw. Nothing. Didn't even bobble his brick of a head atop that mammoth neck. Like slugging a fence post. He hit him again, only this time with his left. Still nothing. Liam low-rumbled through a bloody lip, "You are a dead man, cop."

---

Letty scrambled out of her collapsed tent on all fours, jumped up and faced off with Conor. He hesitated. She figured the take-down was normally Liam Sullivan's job. He must be the *reticent rapist.*

---

Larry parked his car at the trail head. Sprinted up the rough ground toward the watering hole off the AT still a third of a mile away. Halfway there, the sounds of a scuffle echoed through the old-growth forest. And then a single gunshot reverberated through the trees. *Sam's three-five-seven?* His chest screamed at him as he winced and pushed even harder through every excruciating step up that steep mountain trail.

---

Sam absorbed one sledgehammer blow after another from Liam. With his own blows ineffective, he focused on protecting himself as best he could, covering and blocking with his elbows and arms. This was not going well and getting worse fast. On the verge of blacking out from the relentless pounding, he knew the end was near when he spotted this big man once more attempting to snatch his gun close by, but just outside both their grasps. Sam hyper-extended his left arm and covered the butt of the pistol and trigger guard with his own hand and kept it clamped there. But he couldn't pick it up or get it turned to use it, not even as a bludgeon. Still, he had to protect it. Too many cops get shot with their own weapon.

Then, Liam pushed the gun away instead of trying to grab it. Instead, now beneath him, he choked Sam with both hands. Needing a new tactic as his peripheral vision grew grayer, verging on fading to black, Sam reached for Liam's eyes with both of his thumbs as the big man straddled him on the ground. He dug deep. Liam howled, rolled off, and reached for his eyes. Sam pulled himself off the forest floor from the waist up, but despite what his brain commanded, his legs refused to obey.

---

The FBI agents at Smith's cabin were on high alert. They knew that less than two hundred yards north-west and up the mountain from their location, SAC Daniels had reported their two perps were approaching—intent unknown. But they were ordered to hold their position so as not to scare off these two illusive hillbillies by barging in too soon. "Have you ever been anywhere this dark before, Jack?" Marty was the junior agent on this op.

"Yeah, and I sprained an ankle because I couldn't see my feet during a chase. Didn't dare use my flash-light. That would've turned me into a target." Marty chuckled. Jack didn't. He recalled almost dying that night.

That's when everything changed. They heard the distinctive sound of a .357 round echo through the woods. Both jumped as they stood in full tactical gear on the porch of this rustic shelter some come-dian called a cabin. Marty's instinct drove him to turn on his flashlight. Jack hissed at him, "Turn that damn thing off. You'll destroy our night vision." He cracked open the crush-proof Pelican case on the porch deck next to him. Kneeled to extract two pairs of bulky NVGs—Night Vision Goggles. Handed one to Marty and donned the other himself. "How about we use these instead, okay, Marty?" Didn't mean for his tone to sound condescending, but it did. Pushed and held the button until he heard a faint whirring as the battery-powered active optics mechanism came to life.

"Roger that. Sorry."

"Let's go. Orders or not, we're not sitting around while Agent Mather gets her ass shot off by a couple of rednecks."

"But—"

"You got a problem, Agent Barnes?"

"No, you're right. You lead." The kid looked scared. Good.

They started off, but within twenty-five feet, the dense thickets between their location and the fight had them both confused for several minutes before they re-acquired the trail. But after five more minutes, they had found and tramped the wrong trail. "Son-of-a-bitch!" Agent Jack Rasmussen was a city kid. They backtracked in the dim green-gray glow of their NVGs.

Meanwhile, Letty was giving better than she got by evading Conor's onslaught. His body language told her he was frustrated at not being able to put this little bitch down. He confirmed that by saying, "Geez, lady, will ya just stand still?" She popped him with a left/right combo to his nose. Blood spurted everywhere in an impressive flow. She felt the thrill of this tiny victory as she now bobbed and weaved to avoid his grappling in vain.

She then responded, "Why? So you can prove to me what a man you are? You coward." Then, she darted away, and slid back in to bang the palms of both hands on his ears with all the force her wide swing could muster. He screamed in surprise, shook his head, and took a second to recover before charging at her in a bloodthirsty rage.

Once again dodging his onslaught, she recognized this could not last long, as fatigue already slowed her down. She didn't need her profiling skills to recognize Conor's thirst for her death. And right now, both she and Sam seemed to only have defensive options. *We need an offense. But what?* Letty glanced over at Sam, who was on the ground, close to losing consciousness. Juszynska had separated her from her own weapons. Felt like it was all coming apart. *It can't end like this, can it?* She purged such indulgent desperation from her thoughts and focused on how to maneuver back toward the flattened tent and her Glock still inside somewhere. A pair of bullets was the only thing that would stop these freight trains.

And then, as she thought about her life, and how it had come to this, she flashed on vivid memories she'd spent a lifetime burying deep inside. How she and Josie Currant weren't all that different. She blinked her eyes rapidly as this big man came at her again. *Focus, Letty! This isn't over yet.*

# 46

At that very moment, Larry Jamison careened into the campsite like a vengeful whirlwind—out of nowhere. assessed the tactical situation in less than a heart-beat as he ran. Saw one of *the hulks* on the ground rubbing his gouged eyes. Kicked the huge man's head with the merciless force of a fifty-yard field goal attempt. The turd blossom still stumbled back to his feet with his left hand holding his head, the other cross-reached for a huge knife from a sheath on his left hip. Not waiting for him to recover or to draw that blade, Larry delivered a wicked round-house kick to the side of his head. Followed it with a back-kick to the man's sternum with the same foot after a full-circle body pivot. Tagged the big man just beneath his rib cage. Hulk tripped his heel over a tree root, while his knife fell somewhere beyond the dim light's perimeter. On the way down, he reached for anything to stay on his feet. Nothing there.

Larry's head spun. Thought he'd pass out from the excruciating pain caused by his bruised ribs and the exertion of the last hour. Wondered if he'd punctured a lung as he gasped for breath. Rage fueled him now. The glow of an electric camp lantern lay on its side under a collapsed tent. In its subdued glow, he spotted a rock the size of a basketball. Lifted it, but his injured ribs only allowed him to get it to waist-level. So, with whatever reserve of strength he had left, he drop-pushed the small boulder down onto the bad guy's skull. Fucker was done, good and bloody, maybe still alive, but no longer a factor.

Then Larry saw Sam's FBI partner dodging yet another attack from the other mook—thought of him as *Hulk Jr.* She went down. He hustled—more like speed-limped—up behind monster number two now standing over her and clamped a sleeper hold on the big kid. Did his best to avoid those battering ram fists that now flailed around like rocks in a tornado. He took a shot to the side of his head, but it wasn't debilitating. Twenty seconds later, the kid was asleep. Larry dropped him, but stayed standing himself. Somehow. He thought, *Some **kid**. These guys are monsters—in more ways than one.*

In the sudden surreal silence, Larry wheezed to nobody in particular over suddenly slumped shoulders and sagging chest, "How 'bout you pussies get off your asses and cuff these fucks?" He was wheezing hard and loud and cradling his ribs. Doubled over, plopped down on his butt. Tipped over to lie on his side, then on his back, as if he sought a pain-free posture, or had simply decided on a nap. On his back, looking over at their two prisoners, he gaped with incredulity at the bigger one. The kid had a knot as big as a baseball on his now-deformed face. He wheezed, "Why isn't that fucker dead?"

Sam crawled over and zip-tied *Hulk*. Letty did the same to his partner. Retrieved her Glock and stood guard.

As soon as Conor regained full consciousness, it's like the kid couldn't help himself, even though he had to be reeling from Jamison's sleeper hold. He leered at Letty, his speech slurred as he hissed, "*Cunt!*"

Letty didn't laugh in his face, ever the professional; however, she almost surrendered to flinging a few smart-ass remarks of her own. Grabbed the bag these boys had dropped near Letty's tent. Retrieved a roll of duct tape they planned to use on her, tore off a hunk, and slapped it over Conor's filthy mouth, none too gently. He resisted. She stomped his balls, like it was procedure, and turned away. He squealed like a baby pig through his nostrils. Then she stormed over to recover her jacket from her collapsed tent with a bit of a smirk on her bruised face. She rubbed her throat which was raising a nasty welt where Conor had tried to choke her. And her left eye had swollen shut. Didn't matter. She was alive.

Larry and Sam had been observing this tempestuous exchange between Hulk Jr. and Letty. Sam's legs were working again. Larry turned his head back toward Sam, now with Sam's jacket under his head. He gasped for breath every few words, "I like her... even if... she *is* a feeb.... Got stones."

Sam wiped some blood from his nose that was already drying as it mingled with his green and black camo paint. The nasty gash on his scalp bled more, but seemed just too tired to produce much more than a dribble. *Does blood get tired?* He smirked, "That ball-stompin' move a standard FBI subdue procedure, Agent Mather?"

"Nah, just an ad-lib, woods cop." Though her

voice sounded coarse, her warm smile lit up the dim campsite, whose only other illumination came from that battery-powered lantern, still on its side glowing from under the tent. Now shivering and wrapped in her coat, Letty rubbed her gut where Conor had connected. Didn't dare touch her eye, and her throat was now fully inflamed. She still found words of gratitude as she shuffled over to join her fellow warriors. She croaked, "Captain Jamison, I presume. All due respect, sir, where the hell did you come from? Damn glad you did."

Now too weak to talk, still flat on the ground, Larry looked up at her and managed one tiny nod and a waggle-wave from two fingers on his right hand. His eyelids had grown heavy. Sam worried.

# 47

The two FBI agents from the nearby cabin-slash-shelter stumbled into their camp-site with their NVGs swiveled up to take in the after-action chaos. Letty had retrieved her lantern and dialed up its illumination. "Jeez, looks like you guys throw one hell of a party. Agent Mather, you okay?"

"Yeah, Jack, we're fine. Your timing is impeccable. We could use some help."

"It's blacker than a well digger's ass out there. We got turned around. What can we do to aid and assist?"

Letty nodded toward their two prisoners. Jack then nodded toward Travis, but looked confused as he saw the EPO attending to another older guy on the ground. "Sure thing, Letty. Marty, watch over the two body builders over there. Hey, who is this?" He down-nodded toward the older man on his back, wheezing.

Now having trouble talking, Letty forced the words. "Jack, meet Captain Larry Jamison of the Massachusetts Environmental Police, recently escaped from his hospital bed at Berkshire Medical. He's the guy that saved our butts a few minutes ago." Special Agent Jack Rasmussen hoisted his eyebrows, walked over and kneeled beside the exhausted EPO captain. Extended his hand in thanks, but the older guy looked too tired even to raise his arm. All he got was a weak slow-motion wink and a small nod. Jack pulled back his hand. He understood. He said, "Sorry we didn't get here sooner, but we got turned around in that snarl of underbrush out there."

Sam snickered, "That'd be the Mountain Laurel. Brews up a nasty thicket, alright. Like a giant tangle of coarse steel wool laced with razor blades. And your NVGs won't help you get through that stuff. Slick toys, by the way. Must be nice to have that kinda budget." Sam tossed an accusative stare down at his patient and boss. Captain Jamison's eyes remained closed. Lack of a snarky response worried Sam even more.

"Hey, Letty, you Mirandize these animals, yet?"

Letty looked like that was the last thing on her mind. Something snapped. Even though she massaged her now black-and-blue throat, she hoarse-whispered, "No, Jack, we've been too busy staying alive here while you and Marty were enjoying a night hike through the woods. Besides, nobody's asking them any questions, okay?"

"Hey, sorry, already. Jeez, Letty. Don't go all native on me."

"Oh, don't act so bruised, Jack. I just went several rounds with one of these monsters." She nodded over to their two prisoners sitting cross-legged on the ground as she also nursed her sore midsection. "And I'm still amped up. First time, ya know? Different from a desk or a consult."

"No worries, Letty. We get that." He looked embarrassed as he back-peddled. Unceremoniously and unsuccessfully. "You look good all sweaty, though, even though you're all banged up. Held your own," He smiled, thinking he just paid her a compli-ment in a weird post-action sort of way.

"Fuck you, Jack." This time, she didn't apologize for her words. Her hands still shook. Funny what a brush with death does to your psyche.

Sam heard it all, and just smiled.

# 48

They started their long march out after a half-hour of calling in their status and catching their breath. Sam said to the group, "We're gonna meet the troopers at Lower Goose Pond's boat ramp. Once we reported we had two in custody, and our FBI friends were here to help, they're holding their position. Larry, can you walk? Or should we get the EMTs?"

Jamison mumbled under his breath, "Go screw yourself, Sam. Just give me a shoulder to lean on, okay?" He opened his eyes, smiled, and winked at FBI Special Agent Letty Mather.

Sam saw Hulk Jr. roll his eyes, but didn't say a

word. Couldn't with Letty's tape over his mouth. If his hands hadn't been zip-tied behind his back, he'd likely be cradling his sure-to-be-throbbing nuggets if he could reach them. And Hulk Sr.—the bigger one —looked like he got his eggs scrambled from Larry's boulder treatment. His head bobbled like he wasn't all there anymore. Looked at something, but saw nothing. *Concussed? Too damn bad. Rat's game, rat's rules.*

Jack followed protocol. Added handcuffs to Liam's and Conor's plastic cuffs. No way he trusted even stout plastic without stainless steel to back it up.

---

Fifteen minutes later, the six-foot-six Sergeant Samuels met them near the trailhead. The big MSP trooper looked down at the motley crew of five battered, bruised, and bloody bodies limping toward him, escorted by two guys with FBI badges hanging from their jeans pockets with nary a scratch. Samuels said to Sam, "How are you all still alive *and walking*?" He'd been following the radio traffic. Got wide-eyed when he spotted Sam. "Je-ZUS, you look—"

Sam couldn't resist, as he rubbed his bruised

throat and squinted through the dried blood, mud, and the smeared camouflage paint. "Well, Captain Jamison here suggested I have sex with myself before we started our little hike out of the woods. Since it wasn't an order, I respectfully declined, and look at me now." He snorted.

"Say, what?"

"Never mind, Sergeant. We need to get Captain Jamison here into an ambo A-sap. I think he over-exerted himself, saving our bacon back there."

Samuels scratched his forehead beneath the stiff brim of his trooper's hat. "Roger that, Officer Travis. Looks like we need more than one ambulance as well as a prisoner transport. Already en route." He smiled, shook his head from side to side, and waved to another trooper before barking a string of orders. Then, "Why don't y'all sit in our cruisers here till the EMTs arrive to transport you to Berkshire Medical? All warmed up for you. We'll bring your vehicles and take custody of your prisoners." He motioned to four dead-serious troopers who surrounded the two criminals. With his eyes on Travis, Samuels nodded toward the hulks. He said, "Let these two sit in the damn dirt until we escort them to the barracks lock-up and later released to the FBI." He then nodded to the two agents to assure them this was *their* protocol. Please sign the prisoner release forms. Alright, Officer Travis?"

"Deal. All yours. Got anything to drink?"

"Water? Cold thermos coffee about a double-shift old?"

"Anything stronger?"

# 49

The Massachusetts State Police remanded the two prisoners to the FBI after being processed at the MSP barracks in Boston. The satchel that Letty Mather seized at Upper Goose Pond from which she retrieved duct tape to gag Conor Juszynska also contained a necklace: six locks of human hair, four with a small patch of human scalp still attached and in various stages of decomposition. The other two were bound by cheap twine. All hung from a macabre leather lanyard. FBI's crime lab retrieved viable DNA from the lanyard and found a match to one Liam Sullivan. Plus, they identified hair on that necklace that belonged to Doctor Mary Bishop, Geraldine Boettcher, and Josie Currant. That begged the question about three additional victims they hadn't identified. Were any still alive? If not, would their bodies ever be recovered? An intensive interrogation of the two suspects would follow. The identification process of additional victims became a priority to prepare for the trial to come.

The FBI levied federal charges against Sullivan and Juszynska leveraging Agent Letty Mather, EPO Sam Travis, and EPO Larry Jamison as witnesses. Letty gave Sam and Larry credit for the arrest—the *collar*. She also showered Larry with accolades for his *rescue heroics* and persuaded her chain of command to ensure Sam and Larry were central to the prosecution's case. This won Mather a great deal of respect from Travis and Jamison, but it cost her some points within the Bureau. Got accused of parting with Bureau protocol and of *going native*. She claimed it was the right thing to do despite its potential hit to her career. She liked and respected *the Mass E-po boys,* as she called them. Both Captain Lawrence Jamison and EPO Sam Travis received the FBI Medal for Meritorious Service.

. . .

Josie Currant underwent minor cosmetic surgery to graft a patch of scalp to the top of her head. The procedure was successful. She now wears her hair long to hide the spot on the top of her head that refused to grow new hair and was undergoing intensive psychotherapy.

Based on the FBI's recommendation in light of a new discovery, the federal court extradited Sullivan and Juszynska from Massachusetts to be prosecuted in Pennsylvania. That's where it had started nine years earlier, and that's where they found another victim's body—a nine-year-old case, a Jane Doe—once they connected the cases via DNA from Liam's locks-of-hair necklace. Through the subsequent investigation they discovered she was the missing daughter of an influential Pennsylvania state legislator. Same identical MO as revealed when the girl's original case file was reviewed by the FBI, and confirmed when the girl's body was exhumed from a local Potter's Field based on a DNA familial match with her father. That made a total of three bodies found, plus two survivors, and one yet-to-be identified lock of hair from Liam's necklace. The hulks weren't talking.

The state of Pennsylvania now seemed eager to exercise their little-used death penalty for these heinous criminals. They left their rape victims not only brutalized and violated; they relegated them to slow and torturous death by dehydration and exposure. They called *The Trail Predator* crimes "heinous and brutal with especially egregious circumstances."

Once upon a time, Liam and Conor might have been good kids, but they became trapped in a lifetime web of inescapable tragedy. Were they victims of their environment, or merely of bad choices? Didn't matter. The boys had come full circle—they went home to die, back where they started their criminal career. It was time justice was served according to the law. On Friday the 13th of May 1994, Liam Sullivan and Conor Juszynska paid for their crimes and died by lethal injection at SCI Rockview, Pennsylvania after spending almost six years on death row, and after various failed motions and appeals pressed by Pennsylvania human rights groups. This was considered extremely fast.

Ginny Swanson was invited to attend the execution, but declined. She just asked to meet the only other survivor of these *trail predators*, Josie Currant. They bonded and stayed in touch. That would become the genesis of a lifelong friendship. Only they understood the ordeal that six victims suffered.

Against the advice of her therapist, only one

*victim witness* attended execution of this sentence—Josie Currant from Lenox, Massachusetts. She didn't think it was appropriate to smile at the end, so she kept a straight face. Although she *mentally* peed all over the two monsters on the gurneys as they received their just desserts. They just went to sleep. She couldn't help but think they got off too easy. Her therapist said it would be healthy if she prayed for them. So, she prayed they'd be trussed up spread-eagled to a tree of fire in the coldest depths of Hell, and that Satan himself would hurl stinging black gobs of mud at them for all eternity. Amen.

A hiker discovered Doctor Mary Bishop's body the following Spring. She, too, was missing a jagged chunk of her hair and a slice of her scalp. Her husband, while horrified, expressed gratitude for that closure.

---

The press manufactured plenty of headlines:

*"Killer Team Indicted"*
*"Trail Predators To Die"*
*"Is the AT Safe Again?"*

Letty, Sam and Larry had apprehended two serial killers that terrorized thousands of AT hikers and made victims of at least six. National media coverage ensued. Neither the Massachusetts Environmental Police nor the FBI honored these killers with public attention. They also granted no on-camera interviews since they'd likely need to engage in future undercover operations.

Turned out Captain Larry Jamison's rescue heroics that saved the lives of both EPO Sam Travis and Agent Letty Mather, caused one of his bruised ribs to fracture and had punctured his left lung. He recovered under the attentive eye of his old high school sweetheart, Lindsey Magnus. The flame that had been reignited would not be extinguished. Sam remarked his boss seemed like a kid with a crush. Larry remarked, "I ain't no kid, and this ain't no crush, son."

"Well, you old dog. Look at you learning new tricks!"

Larry grinned. Big.

Sam and Kate "officially" moved in together full-time for an indefinite *trial period*. Brian was thrilled and called her 'Mom.' They deferred making wedding plans for the time being.

Looking like three combatants after a major battle, Letty, Sam, and Larry vowed to meet at least annually to celebrate their survival of the *Trail Predators Case*. And to enjoy each other's company, especially after their wounds and bruises and bones healed. Now and then, between those reunions, Larry would remark to Sam, "Don't care what you say, I like that little feeb of yours."

The End?
Nope!

# EPILOGUE

There is a basis in truth for every story in LETHAL TRAIL, including unavoidable violence, actual cases of kidnapping, assault, rape and murder; however, we've made every attempt to tip the scales toward the redeeming qualities of characters and their relationships for the sake of the overall story. We've made every attempt to retain real-world authenticity, even though crafted as a work of hopefully entertaining fiction.

A few factoids:

Capital punishment is legal in Pennsylvania for crimes committed within that state, even though there were only three executions between 1976 and 1999.

---

In the Commonwealth of Massachusetts, County Sheriff's Departments maintain civil law enforcement responsibilities. Criminal law enforcement falls exclusively within the domain of city and state police departments.

---

*The scenario described in Chapter 13 depicts the true story behind these pictures of two Massachusetts Environmental Police Officers rigging the relocation of a large immobilized, but fully conscious black bear, from a tree in a residential neighborhood. You will note the real-world incarnation of Sam Travis, EPO Lt. Tom Kasprzak—co-author of this book— depicted on the right side of this photo.*

Look for the third Sam Travis Adventure called LETHAL BOUNTY, Fall of 2024, a tale that spans two+ centuries in the Berkshire Mountains of Western Massachusetts.

# CAST OF MAJOR CHARACTERS
## IN ALPHABETICAL ORDER

- **Jeff Brahney:** Bank owner/president Wedgewood Community Bank, Wedgewood, Mass. Friend of Sam Travis.
- **Marvin Clearwater: Assistant** Director, FBI's money laundering and forfeiture unit at FBI headquarters in Washington, DC. Jeff Brahney's college friend from Harvard.
- **Pete Dunwoody:** FBI investigator in Marvin Clearwater's Money Laundering and Forfeitures Division.
- **Taxi Fairchild:** Confidential informant
- **Conor Juszynska:** Perpetrator

- **Richard Lowry:** Corrupt DOJ AUSA (Department of Justice Assistant US Attorney)
- **Lindsey Magnus:** Larry Jamison's old high school flame
- **Kim Mason:** Corrupt deep undercover Federal US Fish and Wildlife Service agent
- **Lawrence (Larry) Jamison:** Captain, Massachusetts Environmental Police & Academy Commandant, Framingham, MA
- **Letty Mather:** FBI profiler who becomes Sam's unofficial partner for the *Trail Predators* case
- **Rick Smith:** Lieutenant, Massachusetts State Police, Berkshire County Barracks Commander
- **Roy Stanfield:** Commander MSP CPAC (investigators assigned to the District Attorney's Office)
- **Liam Sullivan:** Perpetrator
- **Sam Travis:** Massachusetts State Environmental Police Officer
- **Tom Verdi:** Massachusetts State Environmental Police Commissioner

# OTHER BOOKS BY GK JURRENS

---

## Historical Fiction (Great Depression Era Crime)

- Black Blizzard: A Lyon County Adventure
- Murder in Purgatory: A Lyon County Mystery

## Aubrey Greigh Mysteries

- Voodoo Vendetta - Culture That Kills
- Dancing With Death - Who Will Die? Or Disappear?

## Sam Travis Adventures:

- Lethal Game - Bears Under Siege

## Contemporary Autobiographical Fiction (Drama)

- Dangerous Dreams: Dream Runners: Book 1
- Fractured Dreams: Dream Runners: Book 2

## Futuristic Fiction (Paranormal Mystery Thrillers)

- **Underground, Mayhem: Book 1**
- **Mean Streets, Mayhem: Book 2**
- **Post Earth, Mayhem: Book 3**
- **A Glimpse of Mayhem: Companion Guide to the Mayhem Trilogy**

### Non-fiction

- **The Poetic Detective: Investigate Rhyme With Reason**
- **Why Write? Why Publish? Passion? Profit? Both?**
- **Moving a Boat and Her Crew**
- **Restoring a Boat and Her Crew**

Turn the page to read an excerpt of Gene's & Tom's new book

LETHAL BOUNTY

# EXCERPT FROM LETHAL BOUNTY

by GK Jurrens and Lt. Tom Kasprzak (retired)
Coming Autumn 2024

Charlestown, Massachusetts
June 17, 1775

Ankle-deep in the blood of their dead and dying compatriots, he and his aide crouched behind a redoubt—one of the earthen barriers his men had hastily constructed on the ridges during the night. Still visible through the dense clouds of smoke in the stagnant air that stung their eyes and burned their lungs, the sun now hung high in the early afternoon sky. It was an otherwise brilliant day.

Despite an incessant hail of musket balls, they bobbed their heads up to risk yet another glance down the hill from their impromptu command post at the advancing British troops. The redcoats were at least double their own numbers, and possessed superior training. Ten yards away with fire in their eyes, the reckless British bastards leapt over mounds of their fallen and advanced with ruthless abandon. *Like they have for the last six-and-a-half hours.* These were battle-hardened professional soldiers of the realm. The young colonel now doubted the wisdom of holding these hills against such a force with the now-dying or already dead farmers and shop-keepers in his own ranks. *This is madness.*

Most of his troops, twelve-hundred strong at the onset, were raw civilians, but harbored a passion for freedom from the oppressive Crown. That passion pounded in their hearts. Those who still lived, anyway. While *this* battle had only been joined at sunrise this day, they were now thrust into the third bloody month of this brutal siege on their own city. They fought to take back their own neighborhoods, their own homes. The new Conti-nental Army dared not relent as long as their fami-lies and friends remained in the clutches of tyrants. Worse, the Crown's considerable occupying force now *terrorized* all of Boston, Middlesex County, and beyond. He shouted over the din of musket fire, now growing more sporadic from their side, "Lads, they've already paid dearly, *far* more than we. In the future, they'll think twice before—"

"Sir, sorry to interrupt," his aide gasped. "Runners are reporting in. Squad leaders report their surviving men have little or no powder remaining. What are your orders, sir?" The aide stood shoulder-to-shoulder with one of the runners. The runner's face of crimson blinked against the blood dripping from his brow into his eyes.

Colonel William Prescott was a man of action, and valor, but also of conscience. He nodded as he wiped the sweat from his brow and addressed his fanatically loyal aide, "The rest of our militia dies here along with General Warren and the others if we do not now retreat. You've done well, boys." He glanced around at his youthful command staff that had mustered in haste. "They'll not soon forget this battle here atop Breed's and Bunker." Then, to the runner and to his aide, "It is time to muster elsewhere and abandon these wretched mounts to the King's ruffians. Order retreat."

His aide saluted. "Yes, sir." At that moment, the left side of his aide's face disappeared into a pink mist.

---

December 1775

Dark and dangerous times. Most were beyond exhaustion, on the verge of starvation, already victims of exposure. Few men were to be trusted. The same could be said of Mother Nature in her brutal splendor. Early December in Western Massachusetts would not suffer fools. Snow refused to fall. Only a smattering of fickle ice crystals floated earthward. One touched down on Henry's nose, but refused to melt. He saw it land, but felt nothing. Now, he stood stiff on a frozen hill in this... wilderness. He was not alone, but stood apart.

A few short months ago, this quiet twenty-five-year-old bookseller from Boston was thrust into the role of rebel warrior and leader. That meant absorbing a great deal of responsibility almost overnight with very little knowledge or experience. And now, he wondered, *Am I up to this monumental task? Circumstance begs my destiny, and I do possess a damn good nose for this bloody business. At least the General thinks so.* Lucy understood. Henry missed her sorely. On this bitter evening, he found himself on the fringe of nowhere, wondering how he had come to this. But he knew. He'd have it no other way.

He longed to smell the pungent smoke of fires in the encampment, but the men could find no dry wood. Instead, they welcomed the stench of cow cakes from their few oxen and almost two-hundred-fifty horses. They offered precious packets of steamy warmth. Not so long ago, as a civilized city boy, he'd have turned his nose away from such vulgarity—no longer. He gazed down the gentle slope to the nearest stout sled fifty paces distant. It bent under the weight of a six-thousand-pound mortar, recently the property of His Bloody Majesty, strapped to its oaken frame with iron gussets. No amount of gold could fetch that carriage's worth this night. Nor a king's ransom. Not even with the life's blood of every last man in his care—all one hundred and forty-three souls. *Can I live with such a charge? I must.*

Tensions between the Crown and the colonies had been simmering, en route to a full boil for these last five years. It came to a head the previous spring. He was a lieutenant then, an active member of the Massachusetts militia that supported the Patriot provisional government. That was dangerous enough. Under cover of darkness and civilian attire,

Henry had snuck around side streets and alleyways in his beloved Boston. He'd hid his colors to fight with naught but his wit and daring. The oppression the Crown now imposed upon everyone and every-thing he held dear suffocated him. He especially feared for his Lucy. Dearest Luce *never* felt safe anymore. All because the Crown wished to recoup its enormous financial losses in the North American theater of war. Their fight with the French over conquest of territory in the Americas exploded England's national debt. So, they levied an unending stream of taxes on its colonies. Enforcing these levies grew violent. The colonials fought with feroc-ity. They resisted paying for the Brits' war in Quebec and elsewhere. If only freedom were free....

Five years earlier, at twenty, Henry had witnessed the senseless massacre of a half-dozen friends and acquaintances in his own Boston neighborhood. These same thugs in their preten-tious blood-red waistcoats, the King's regulars, had gone mad. They murdered people he knew right in front of his bookstore, not ten paces from his store's windows. An unquenchable thirst for power had gone to their heads with the King's blessing, thinking they could do anything they wanted to these unwashed masses, these... *colo-nials*. Pompous brutes with a bloodlust, Henry had stood strong between a row of long guns and his friends—those who still lived. Barely beyond his teens, he had attempted to play the role of diplomat, talking down one bloodthirsty captain, an arrogant Grenadier who obviously loathed being relegated to menial crowd suppression. Especially this far from the Crown. Since then, the time for diplomacy had dissipated in endless clouds of musket smoke.

During his covert days, Henry had gathered intelligence he had used to save scarce Colonial military supplies from being confiscated by a squad of British thugs, barely escaping with his life. His compatriots recognized him for his cleverness as a quiet man who stood firm behind the more brazen members of the resistance. Rowdies like Revere and Prescott. Unlike them, Henry avoided the more lively subversions, like that massacre on Breed's Hill— they *should* have fought from atop Bunker's higher elevation, not Breed's more forward position. That was even the plan. Reckless ruffians, but Henry was glad they were on their side. With ever-escalating violence across Middlesex County and Massachusetts Bay, Boston had become an urban battle zone. So, he and Lucy fled to regroup with those of like minds as open hostilities, now far more deadly and more frequent than occasional street skirmishes, prevailed across the city. And across their beloved colonies.

Shaken from his reverie, the bitter December wind inspired an involuntary full-body shiver. Henry's black knee-high Wellingtons were handsome boots, though now scuffed to raw hide, not so long ago fashionably appropriate for traversing Boston's finer cobble-paved neighborhoods. But they now did little to forestall inevitable frostbite in this forsaken wilderness, even with extra cotton stuffed in their toe boxes. Many of his men weren't so lucky. Some marched barefoot. Some left bloody trails in the light snow. Though his command was one of the Colonial Army's few artillery units called *The Train*, few of Henry's men wore any sort of uniform. Most layered much of the clothing they owned against the weather. His and the General's primary charge was to keep this rag-tag group of rebels from quitting. He now worried as the train became scattered, worried that some men might just make for their home-steads. He worried without end.

Henry Knox lied to himself that smoking his pipe might warm him against the night, even if just a bit. Though frigid to the bone, he burned with patriotic fervor; however, he continued to worry about his train of sleds. He drew deep into his lungs harsh

Maryland tobacco smoke from his *little ladle,* his treasured but oh, so fragile clay pipe. Exhaled as tendrils swirled out of his nostrils and rose into the moonlight. Of course, the rigors of a winter march resulted in more than one chip at the end of the pipe's short stem. But that pipe was one of his most treasured and well-guarded possessions out here in this frigid field. *Nothing in all the world like the scent of the pipe on a forbidding eve.*

Henry's brother, William, whispered as they stood close, shoulder to shoulder. Their vast encampment dared not risk discovery. Henry smiled. *Whispering* amid their massive gathering comprising dozens of oxen and one-hundred-twenty-four teams of horses to transport forty-two sleds carrying fifty-eight cannons, howitzers, and mortars from Fort Ticonderoga to Boston? Silly to whisper, but he resisted disparaging his dear younger brother's conscientious effort at unnecessary discretion. "Henry, if we are found out, we surely shall face a firing squad."

"No, William, we will not. This is the time to make our stand. If we do not, history will judge us harshly. The very success of General Washington's endeavors on behalf of the Continental Army may very well depend on us completing our task. The General awaits our artillery in desperation. Besides, firing squads are for traitors. We are patriots, stewards of our precious rebellion."

---

They'd been on the road for a month-and-a-half already, bone-tired and lower than ever on supplies. The men were dying of exposure and despair. The weather? Worse than abominable. Still, Henry wished for more of the same. He *needed* snow to grease the skids of his sleds. Most of the men wrapped neckerchiefs over the top of their heads to protect their ears from the biting wind. No fancy tricorns or cocked hats for this bunch. Wool caps were a precious and rare commodity. Those lucky enough to own or commandeer a second kerchief or scarf also bundled their frost-bitten faces. And the temperature would continue to plummet if the evening's sky offered a portent of their near future. It was Henry's responsibility to find shelter, and he had failed.

So, they camped scattered alongside the wooded trail where dense stands of spruce and hemlock offered a wind break, at least. The men slept in their bedrolls close to the beasts of burden and the steaming body heat they radiated. The sleds carried not only machines of war, but feedbags. They, too, now collapsed flat—near empty. Worse, with almost no grass visible through the light snow, grazing prospects remained grim. Henry already had lost half of his few oxen reserved for the heaviest of their forty-two sleds, with but two to spare. And most of the horses had lost weight and muscle. Although his teamsters suffered alongside their hungry beasts, they would not complain.

Even though money was in short supply, Henry found a farmer yesterday willing to accept Continentals. The new Continental currency sufficed in lieu of Colonial money, or British pounds, or Spanish coins. They saved their doubloons and other coinage when nothing else sufficed. Henry had purchased a half-dozen oxen from that farmer, but then he learned with surprise that their financial larder was significantly depleted. Truth be told, he wasn't much of an accountant. He'd talk with his purser, Sergeant Grossman.

Now, here he was, an artillery colonel in the Continental Army, with the constant threat of confronting the finest soldiers in the world—British regulars. That was a daunting prospect in itself. But *also* dreaded Hessian auxiliaries—world-class mercenaries—were known to be employed by the British in conflicts such as theirs. According to the

General, the Crown favored using these experienced soldiers in their conflicts elsewhere. It was only a matter of time.

Worse, with loyalties divided within almost every household, every action questioned, and not knowing who might be a British collaborator or spy, no one was to be trusted. *For the love of God, what is keeping us from lying down and drifting off in peaceful slumber?* But no. The General needed him and his train. As General Washington implored him in a recent correspondence, "the want of them is so great, that no trouble or expence [sic] must be spared to obtain them." And he *was* obtaining them.

William asked, "We *are* doing the right thing, aren't we, Henry? I mean, Colonel?"

Contrary to his own conflicted thoughts, Colonel Knox's condescending glance at his younger brother left no doubt. "William, it is true General Washington has only been in command of the Continental Army since July. And our beloved rebellion *is* only a few months old." He surveyed the vast field of captured British armament before him, now in his charge. "But if our commander-in-chief doesn't have this artillery for his purposes in the bulwarks around Boston, our entire noble effort might be in vain. Then, my dearest brother, the Crown will charge you, me, and every man in this company with treason. And they *will* shoot us *if* we make it as far as a firing squad. There is no more hiding. But that does *not* mean we are traitors, only that we are rebels, no longer willing to kiss King George's ring or bend the knee to his royal arse." He hadn't intended his voice to raise in pitch and volume. Theirs was a righteous cause, and he would not accept any doubt whatsoever. William appeared reassured, but Henry thought, *If only my own confidence matched my words.*

They had left Boston six weeks earlier for a secret meeting with one of General Washington's cohorts. Henry, William, and only a squad of Grenadiers had followed the coast south to New York City. After meeting with Major General Schuyler in New York, they then possessed the funds for their expedition. It wasn't much, but perhaps enough to save the fledgling rebellion. They then headed north along the Hudson for a brief stop in Albany. From there, they continued due north to the captured Fort Ticonderoga, where the rest of his command awaited their arrival.

Colonel Knox and his soldiers spent three precious days collecting all the heavy weapons they could gather on a landing at Lake George. It was called Fort George, but was little more than a collection of cabins perched on the lake's shore, guarded by a handful of sentries. The camp didn't even feature a perimeter fence. Not yet, anyway. Their best security remained their obscure location.

In a brief but bloody skirmish, Ethan Allen and the militia he called his Green Mountain Boys had captured Fort Ticonderoga. They discovered the British had all but abandoned the fort just weeks earlier, including an armory deemed too difficult to move with any rapidity. Now, General Washington intended to use those same weapons to eject the admiralty fleet from Boston. Failing to do so, however, could very well spell the end of their noble quest. Henry reminded himself once more, *The General—my friend—is depending on **me**. And the very survival of our revolution may well hang in the precarious balance.*

\*\*\*

Abraham and Jacob Jenkins huddled together against the night wind as they watched the young colonel and his even younger brother up on the hill, smoking. Of course, *they* had tobacco. Food, too, they wagered. The stench of cow cakes from a big steaming ox standing over them offered a welcomed though meager source of temporary heat. They did not fear being trampled. The oxen appeared frozen in place after a long day of hauling the heaviest sleds. Abe snarled, "I know where they keep the money, Jake."

"But if we get caught, they'll shoot us, sure." Jake kept his hands stuck down the front of his trousers for the warmth. He huddled with his older brother.

"So we don't get caught, Jake. 'Sides, they won't even miss it."

The next morning, the company pressed on. The brothers Jenkins bided their time. They had grown weary of this fool's errand of suffering and dying for nothing, anyway.

---

If you're enjoying this sample of *Lethal Bounty*, look for it on Amazon and elsewhere Autumn 2024.

# DISCLAIMER

**Although this tale is based on a true story, this is a work of fiction. Any similarity to actual persons, behaviors, places or events should be considered coincidental and fictional.**

No part of this publication may be stored in a retrieval system, transmitted, used by any AI system, or reproduced in any way, including, but not limited to, digital copying and printing without prior agreement and written permission of the publisher, UpLife Press.

Research of this manuscript's period and its theme mandated judicious use of ethnic pejoratives and mild profanity and are not meant to offend the reader. Quite the contrary, the use of these literary devices is intended to demonstrate a commitment to authenticity.

# DEDICATION

*We dedicate this story to the officers of the law who protect us, day after day, year after year. They, too, pay a toll for providing this essential service to our communities.*

*But we especially acknowledge the victims of crimes, their families, and friends. We dedicate this story—their story—to them.*

# ACKNOWLEDGMENTS

To my friend, Tom Kasprzak
and to all our beta readers and technical advisors.
I thank you for being part of the team.

We thank all of our Sam Travis fans. Without you,
there is no story.

# BEFORE YOU GO

*Please post a brief review on Amazon.*

*Or email your thoughts to gjurrens@yahoo.com.*
Remember, other readers and we need to know
what you think.
**I absolutely read every single review with
gratitude.**
**Thank you.**

Also, feel free to browse or subscribe at
GKJurrens.com for announcements and giveaways.
See you there!

GK

# ABOUT THE AUTHOR

GK Jurrens writes with undiluted passion, having published a dozen fiction and non-fiction titles to date, including ten novels. He also teaches writing and independent publishing nationwide.

GK and his wife live and travel in a motorhome. They wander their beloved North America as a source of endless inspiration.

After studying Liberal Arts and Electronics Engineering Technology, GK earned a Bachelor of Science degree in Business and a Master of Science degree in Management of Technology from the University of Minnesota, USA.

Six years of government service and a successful three-decade career in global high-technology preceded more than a few years of sailing America's waterways, the Florida Keys, and the Eastern Caribbean from the British Virgin Islands to Granada, near the coasts of Venezuela and Trinidad. Plus, brief forays sailing around the Greek Cyclades

Islands in the Aegean Sea and the San Juan Islands in the American Pacific Northwest.

GK now pursues his life-long penchant for the creative arts: prose and poetry, painting (watercolor), traveling (North America), playing guitar and his growing collection of Native American style flutes, some of which he crafted while living in the Arizona desert. This is also where he acquired a passion for learning to play the impossible ancient pueblo flutes and the Japanese bamboo flute called the Shakuhachi.

He enjoys quiet evenings reading and exploring movies, when not writing or sitting by a campfire alongside his copilot and soulmate of over half a century—'Admiral' Kay.

If you'd care to offer the author feedback, for which he'd be grateful, consider emailing **gjur rens@yahoo.com** or visit **GKJurrens.com** and subscribe.

facebook.com/genejurrens

instagram.com/gjurrens

linkedin.com/in/gkjurrens

# ABOUT TOM KASPRZAK

Meet the real-world version of Sam Travis, and major contributor to the Sam Travis Adventure Series, Lieutenant Tom Kasprzak (retired). "LT" spent thirty-two years as an environmental police officer for the Commonwealth of Massachusetts. Before graduating in 1977 from the Massachusetts State Police Academy, Tom earned the coveted "top gun" award for superior marksmanship.

Before his law enforcement career, Tom served in the US Air Force during the Viet Nam War. He was then assigned to the 9th Strategic Reconnaissance Wing the home of the famed SR-71 Blackbird spy plane and worked with Command Staff in the Special Security Office.

He began his EPO career as a field officer in various assignments involving both inland and marine enforcement in places like Cape Cod, Boston Harbor and others. After transferring to the Berkshire Mountains in Western Massachusetts with skills honed from 7+ years of varied case involvement and courtroom testimony, he forged close relationships with local and state police.

Upon being promoted to lieutenant, he led a region of officers in search and rescue operations involving plane crashes, boating fatalities, narcotics, and the investigation and apprehension of various firearm violators.

Beginning in 1986, LT engaged in undercover or supervised undercover operations focused on endangered wildlife. During that time, he worked with other local, state, and federal agencies on issues ranging from the environment to anti-terrorism.

Tom was selected to train in no fewer than three extended tours at the prestigious Federal Law Enforcement Training Center (FLETC) in Glynco, Georgia, where federal law enforcement agencies train.

Those intensive and immersive training tours honed his skills for inter-agency undercover operations, marine operations, and advanced operational readiness. He also trained for, and was an Incident Commander in several cases.

During his colorful career, Tom worked with the Massachusetts State Police air wing on helicopter operations, their dive team, apprehension team, marine law enforcement, and environmental police operations.

Tom spent his last seven years assigned to the State Police STOP (apprehension) team headquarters in Chicopee, Massachusetts, along with all the members of the region he supervised.

His undercover assignments brought dozens of individuals to justice who violated state and federal laws. He was also a Deputy National Marine Fisheries agent, as well as a U.S Deputy Fish and Wildlife agent at the same time.

His largest case—Operation Berkshire—closed one of the country's largest illegal commercial wildlife trafficking operations involving twenty-nine individuals, six states and two foreign countries.

The exploits of Tom and his fellow officers from his home state and others led to new exploits in crusading against illegal wildlife commercialization.

*National Geographic produced a special called "Wildlife Wars: Bears Under Siege" that featured Tom and his fellow undercover operatives after they closed Operation Berkshire.*

Tom taught new recruits at the State Police Academy courses in courtroom procedures, officer ethics and undercover operations. He also delivered endangered species lectures to schools, colleges, municipal police departments, as well as to other state and federal agencies including US Coast Guard

District One in Boston with whom he was specifically trained in LNG (Liquid Natural Gas) tanker escort anti-terrorism protocols in Boston Harbor.

He made a name for himself during dozens of successful missing persons, body recovery cases, undercover operations, anti-terrorism and crime scene investigations. Tom and his life partner, Karen, now split their time between Western Massachusetts and Southwestern Florida.